Love Lost, Love Found

By William Speir

Names, characters, businesses, places, events, and incidents are either the products of the author's imagination or used in a fictitious manner. Any resemblance to actual persons, living or dead, or actual events, is purely coincidental.

No part of this publication may be reproduced, stored in a retrieval system, or transmitted in any form or by any means, electronic, mechanical, photocopying, recording, or otherwise, without the written permission of the publisher.

Text Copyright © 2023 William Speir

All rights reserved.
Published 2023 by Progressive Rising Phoenix Press, LLC
www.progressiverisingphoenix.com

ISBN: 978-1-958640-43-2

Printed in the U.S.A.
1st Printing

Cover Photograph: "Just Married Couple Kissing On Tropical Beach At Sunset" by EpicStockMedia, ShutterStock Photo ID: 168554681, used under license from ShutterStock.com.

Interior Illustration: "Sydney" by TheMumins, ShutterStock Vector ID: 108969926, used under license from ShutterStock.com.

Book and Cover design by William Speir
Visit: http://www.williamspeir.com

To my Bonnie Lass, the love of my life, my best friend, and my partner through all the seasons of our lives. This is part your story, and it's part their story. Thank you, Sweetheart, for the best years of my life!

PROLOGUE

Natalie Patterson sat on the edge of her bed in the house she shared with her older brother, Ed. It was early March in Brisbane, the capital of Queensland, Australia. Natalie was wearing a pair of exercise shorts along with her favorite pair of sandals. She was also wearing a snug, ribbed singlet (tank top), which accentuated her ample breasts. She knew that the tight shirt and exposed legs might be a distraction for her soon-to-be-ex-boyfriend, but she had a long drive ahead of her, and comfort was her primary concern.

The walls of her bedroom were bare, the bed had been stripped, and everything she owned was in boxes piled in the hallway by the front door. She could hear Ed taking the boxes out and placing them in the back of her car. Through the bedroom window, she could see the smoke rising from Ed's fire-pit, where the photos of Amir were burning in the morning light.

Natalie was a striking young woman who had just turned twenty-three years old. Her long, straight, light-brown hair hung down, shrouding her face as she stared at her phone, dreading the text that she knew she needed to send. Her large brown eyes were still wet from crying, which she had been doing for nearly a week—ever since Amir had done the unforgivable, which was really saying something, given the number of times Natalie had forgiven him before and taken him back, foolishly believing him when he said he'd never do anything so terrible again.

Deciding that she couldn't put it off any longer, and knowing that she had a long drive ahead of her, she opened the Messenger app on her phone and started typing what she hoped was her last text to Amir.

Amir, I'm ready to talk. Come to my brother's house. If you're not here in 30 minutes, I won't be either.
Natalie

Natalie had first met Amir Dimitrios at a party four years earlier, during her first year at university. He was three years older, completing his degree and preparing to start his first post-graduate degree program. Her straight hair was sun-bleached back then, and the short summer dress she wore showed off her lean, taut legs. She was immediately attracted to his tall, lean build and his half-Greek, half-Lebanese features. He was taken by her slim yoga-aficionado's figure, big beautiful eyes, and wide smile, which lit up the room.

They arranged to meet for coffee two days later. After that, they got together at least three times a week. She fell for him hard, and it wasn't long before they became lovers—at her initiation. In fact, as Natalie was to realize later, everything related to their relationship—whether emotional or physical—had been initiated by her and not by Amir.

Amir was a prankster and had been since a child. But in the age of the internet and sophisticated video technology, what he referred to as "pranks" became more about filming the reactions of the person being pranked so Amir could post the videos on the internet. Amir had a loyal group of followers for his videos, and when Natalie started appearing in the videos with him, the number of subscribers went up from a few thousand to over two million.

At first, Amir and Natalie would play pranks on Amir's friends. The pranks were harmless and all in good fun. After a while, Natalie became the target of some of the pranks. She enjoyed most of them, and the two had a good laugh once the prank had been revealed. But some went a bit too far, leaving Natalie an emotional wreck for days.

When Natalie didn't appreciate the "humor" of the prank, Amir was quick to apologize, swearing that he'd never do it again. Then he'd shower Natalie with gifts until she forgave him. She would, and everything would be wonderful... until he thought of a new and more extreme way to prank her.

One prank, which to Natalie wasn't a prank at all and left her shaking for days, involved having her watch as Amir put her car into a car crusher and smashed it into a small cube, before presenting her with a new car. Amir had a great deal of money, and while Natalie never knew the source, she had been the recipient of his generosity many times. It was his generosity that kept her from recognizing the patterns of abusive behavior and how she was allowing herself to be manipulated.

After a while, Natalie began striking back at Amir. He'd prank her, she'd retaliate, and he'd escalate. He was definitely someone who could "dish it out, but not take it." After a couple of years of this, Natalie realized that pranking and *doing the naughty*—as she and her girlfriends referred to sex—were all they really shared, and it wasn't enough for her anymore. She wanted to be in a loving, committed relationship with a mature man, not some immature man-boy who considered manipulation and love to be the same thing. Every beautiful thing he did for her was tied to a video—either giving her a gift as part of the prank, or to earn forgiveness for a prank that went wrong. Natalie began to see that their relationship was just about internet content—entertaining his fans and getting likes for his videos.

Love Lost, Love Found

She was more of an accessory than a girlfriend, and she was growing tired of being a prop.

Amir's temper was also becoming an issue for Natalie. If she agreed with him, or if she reacted to a prank the way he wanted, he was fine. If she disagreed, or if she did something different from what he wanted, he'd shout at her until she backed down. And if she didn't back down, he'd stomp around threateningly. He never hit her, but what he did was bad enough to scare her.

When Natalie finished university with a Business Management/Commerce degree—her major was International Business—from the University of Queensland, she had to decide if she should start her career or stay in university and get a Master's Degree. Amir didn't like either of these options because of the time they would take Natalie away from him.

The one person Natalie could always talk to was her brother, Ed. He lived near the university and didn't hesitate to invite Natalie to move into his home to be closer to the campus. He didn't charge her rent, but he did ask that she help with the cooking and cleaning, which she happily did.

Natalie and Ed spent hours talking every week, and while he did his best not to interfere in her relationship with Amir, Ed did listen to Natalie as she talked about her growing frustrations with the man-boy she'd been with for four years.

"He doesn't want me to stay in uni to get a master's degree," she lamented one night in September, "and he doesn't want me to get a job in marketing. So today, I got a job as a receptionist with a local company just so I have some money coming in. I have *got* to figure out what to do with my life. I feel like my world is revolving around Amir, like he's the center of the universe or something, and I'm really starting to hate it.

Shouldn't there be more to life than just filling *his* needs?"

Ed nodded sympathetically. "Do you at least like the work?" he asked.

"I hate it," she exclaimed. "It sucks, my manager sucks, the whole company sucks. It's just a paycheck, and they treat me like dirt."

"Isn't that how Amir treats you, too?" Ed probed.

Natalie glared at him. "Sometimes." She looked down in shame. "Most of the time, actually. Ed, what am I going to do?"

"Start putting yourself first," Ed told her. "Stop living your life around what others want from you and start living the life *you* want to. If people object, they don't deserve to be in your life. If they support you, then those are your people."

Natalie thought about this. "Do you know what I actually want to do?"

"What?"

"I want to work abroad… in another country. Get out of Australia and start fresh somewhere else."

Ed's eyes went wide. "Seriously?"

Natalie nodded.

"Then you should pursue that," Ed stated.

"And if I lose Amir because my life pulls me away from him?"

"Then I say good riddance," Ed stated. "Your life can't be all about him, Natalie. This is *your* life we're talking about, not his. It's time you stop living on other people's terms."

A few days later, Natalie saw a notice on the uni's job board that a large international marketing firm, based in the United States, was looking for interns. The internships would last a year, and at the end, the interns who performed the best would receive permanent job offers. Natalie showed the notice to Ed when he

Love Lost, Love Found

got home from work that night.

"This could be a great way to jump-start my career," she said after he read the notice.

"What does Amir think about this?" Ed asked.

"I haven't shown him yet," she confessed. "This could be a way to get some distance from Amir while I figure out my... my future. Besides, Amir will be in the final year of his second Master's degree, so he won't have much time for me anyway. The timing could be perfect."

"You'll have to tell him at some point," Ed pointed out.

"I know," Natalie agreed. "But I want your opinion first."

Ed looked at the notice again. "America, eh? Are you sure you want to move half-way around the world just for a fresh start in life?"

"I don't seem able to pursue my own dreams staying around here, do I? I need a change, and I need space. And I need some adventure. I feel trapped right now, and if I don't break out soon, I'll never be able to."

Ed looked at his sister. "Then go for it. Do what you have to do to find what you want in life. To hell with what Amir thinks."

Natalie went to Amir's house the next evening. She was honest with him about the internship and her desire to pursue it.

Oddly enough, Amir didn't say anything to discourage her. In fact, he barely said anything at all.

"He didn't object?" Ed asked when Natalie got home later that night.

"No. I don't know if he was too distracted by the video he was editing to actually listen, or if he didn't think I'd ever pursue something out of the country. But it doesn't matter. I've made up my mind. I'm applying for the internship."

Natalie sent in her application, and after three video

interviews, she was accepted into the internship program.

Because the internship was in the United States, Natalie had to apply for an immigration and work visa from the United States Consulate in Sydney. This required stacks of paperwork to be completed and submitted, medical examinations, and an in-person interview with a Consulate official. Natalie scheduled the interview, hoping that there would be no issues with her paperwork and application.

When Natalie told Amir that she had been accepted into the internship program and was following the steps necessary to get her visa to live and work in America, he was livid.

"What the hell, Natalie! What do you mean you're going to work in America for a year?"

"We talked about this, Amir," Natalie reminded him. "You weren't supportive, but you didn't tell me not to pursue it. Besides, you're going to be busy for the next year finishing your second Master's Degree, and you're not going to have that much time for us anyway. I need to do this for me, Amir, just like your second Master's is something you need to do for you. Why shouldn't I have the same opportunity as you?"

"But what about the video channel?" Amir demanded. "I can't just put that on hold for a year until you get back. And what if they offer you a permanent position over there? What'll that do to us?"

"If they offer me a permanent job, I'll have to see where I am with my career when and if that happens. As for the video channel, it'll be nice not be the victim of one of your pranks for a whole year. Seems like a winner to me."

"You're not taking the internship, and that's final," Amir shouted. "I won't let you."

"You don't own me, Amir." Natalie said icily, standing her ground. "And I'll take the internship or any other job that I feel is in *my* best interest. You can either be supportive or not, but I'm going to do what's best for me."

Love Lost, Love Found

"And what about our trip to Seoul for the conference?" Amir demanded.

"What conference in Seoul?"

"The conference for video content creators. I told you about it weeks ago. I've already booked our flights and got our hotel reservations. You agreed to go with me, remember?"

"How can I remember what you never told me, Amir? What are the dates?"

Amir told her what day they were leaving and when they were coming back.

"Send that to me, and I'll check my schedule."

"What do you mean by that?" Amir demanded.

"Just what it sounds like," Natalie stated. "I'll check my schedule and see if I can go with you or not."

Amir didn't take Natalie's response well. But no matter how much he yelled at her, she wouldn't back down.

Later that night, after Natalie was asleep, Amir took matters into his own hands. He didn't want her to be accepted into the internship program or be granted a U.S. visa. He wanted Natalie with him in Seoul, because of the attention he got when she was on his arm, and he didn't want her to be away from him, even though he'd be busy for the next year finishing his latest degree. He slipped out of bed, took her phone, and hacked her calendar app. He changed the date of the Consulate interview to the following week and added the conference in Seoul.

When Natalie got home the next morning, Ed was waiting for her.

"How did it go with Amir?" he asked.

"How do you think?" Natalie grumbled.

"That bad?"

"Worse. He *forbade* me to take the internship. He's furious about me being gone for a whole year… or more if I get offered a permanent job."

"Are you going to let that stop you?" Ed asked.

Natalie shook her head. "No, I'm more convinced than ever that it's the right thing to do, no matter what Amir says or does."

Natalie heard a chime on her phone and checked her text messages. It was a message from Amir about the trip to Seoul. She checked her calendar and saw that she already had the trip set up. *I guess he did tell me and I just didn't remember.* She saw that it was the week before her interview at the U.S. Consulate. *I guess I can go with him without risking my Consulate interview. Who knows… it might be fun.* She sent Amir a text confirming that she'd go with him to Seoul.

Natalie and Amir flew to South Korea. These conferences were non-stop parties, networking opportunities, and workshops about keeping video content fresh and interesting. Amir went to a few of the workshops, but Natalie mostly hit the parties and hung out with the other women attendees.

On the second day of the conference, Natalie received an email from the U.S. Consulate stating she had missed the interview. "What? What?" she exclaimed aloud. "How is that possible? The interview isn't until next week."

Confused, Natalie raced back to the hotel room to call the Consulate and find out what was going on. When she reached the Consular official she was supposed to meet with, she asked why she had received the email.

"Your interview was this morning, Miss Patterson," the official told her. "Since you missed the interview, we cannot process your visa application."

"But my calendar says that the interview is next week," Natalie protested. "I'm in Seoul, South Korea, right now. Is there any way we can reschedule?"

There was a long pause. Then the official said, "I'll see what I have available. Call me when you get back from South Korea, and we'll see what can be done."

Natalie stared at the hotel room wall, stunned. *I would never have come to Seoul if the interview was this week.* Then Natalie remembered how she didn't think Amir had ever told her about the trip to South Korea. *Did Amir hack my phone and change my calendar?* She checked her email and found the original confirmation for the interview. It showed that the official had been right. The interview had been scheduled for that morning.

I know I entered the information correctly in my calendar. Amir did this. He didn't want me to get my visa, so he torpedoed my Consulate interview. That son-of-a-bitch!

She saw that a new email had arrived from the company that had offered her the internship. She opened it and read:

Dear Miss Patterson, We were notified that you missed your Consulate interview this morning, which is required to obtain a visa so you can work in the United States. Without a visa, it is not possible for you to be part of the internship program. Therefore, we have no choice but to rescind our offer.

Natalie was devastated. *He tricked me into coming here with him, and it cost me the internship. I have to fix this. He's not going to get away with screwing up my life anymore.*

Enraged, she called the airline and rescheduled her flight home. There was an opening on a flight leaving Seoul for Brisbane in three hours. Natalie booked the flight. Then she called Ed and asked him to pick her up at the airport.

"Why are you coming home so early?" Ed asked. "And why isn't Amir coming home with you?"

Natalie explained what had happened.

"That piece of crap!" Ed said. "I'll be at the airport waiting for you. What are you going to do about your visa and the internship?"

"I don't know, but I'll find a way to make this right," Natalie vowed.

As soon as Natalie was back in Australia, she worked to reschedule the interview with the U.S. Consulate while trying to get the internship program offer reinstated. The company in America finally agreed to let her back into the program, but they told her that the final offer would depend not only on the successful grant of a visa by the State Department, but on an in-person assessment of her as a candidate by one of their top people, who was scheduled to be in Australia in May. Natalie agreed to the terms and conditions.

"Can you believe I have to wait until May to find out if I get the internship after all?" Natalie asked Ed when she told him about what was happening.

"At least they're still willing to consider you," Ed said. "That's a good sign."

Natalie nodded. She looked at her phone, saw that Amir was calling her again, and hit the button on her phone to reject the call.

"Amir again?"

"Yes. He's called and texted non-stop since I left Korea. He's stuck there until the conference is over, so at least I don't have to see him for another couple of days. But he'll be back here tomorrow. I'll have to do something, but not yet."

"When are you going to talk to him?"

"Soon," Natalie said. "But it'll be in person. And I've already decided what I'm going to do."

"Which is?"

"I'm breaking up with that son-of-a-bitch. He wants to repair the damage he's done to our relationship, but there's no chance of that. This is... unforgivable. And get this... he's furious that I left Korea without him. It never occurred to him that I'd be mad about what he did—either that, or he doesn't believe that I know he's the one who changed my calendar. By the way, I'm moving to Sydney to get away from him. Aunt Rachel is letting me move in with her, and she's giving me a job at her shop. I need some distance and some peace from Amir, and I need to be closer to the U.S. Consulate in case they need any additional information from me. Plus, the guy from America who's assessing me will be in Sydney, so I need to be there when he arrives."

"I think that's a good idea, Sis. I'll miss you, but it's a good idea. You'll have fun with Aunt Rachel. She's more like a big sister to you, anyway. And it's a good thing that Amir doesn't know her well or where she lives down there."

Ed noticed a strange look in Natalie's eyes. "What's going on, Sis? There's more that you're not telling me."

Natalie nodded. "It's interesting what you can see clearly when you're away from someone. I've been away from Amir for several days, and I'm already seeing things that I never noticed before."

"Like what?" Ed asked.

"Like the patterns of emotional abuse he's subjected me to for the past four years. He's never crossed the line to physical abuse, but I can see how he manipulated me and emotionally— psychologically—abused me for years. And it's not just the pranks. It's the whole pattern of our relationship. I've got to be free of him while there's still enough of me left."

"Then why meet with him in person?" Ed asked. "Why give him the chance to manipulate you again?"

"Because I'm going to show him the respect that he never showed me. I'm not going to stoop to his level. I'll have him come over the morning I'm leaving for Sydney. It'll be the last time he sees me. And trust me, there's no way he can convince me to stay. I'll tell him it's over, and then I'm out of here."

Amir pulled into Ed's driveway twenty-five minutes after he got Natalie's text. He had been at the gym, so he was wearing his workout clothes and was sweaty; for some reason, Amir was always sweaty. As he got out of his car, he saw Ed loading boxes into Natalie's car, but it didn't register what Ed was actually doing. Amir waved a greeting and ran up the front steps of Ed's house. The front door was open, and when Amir reached the entrance, he turned and asked, "Is it all right if I go inside?"

Ed nodded. "She's waiting for you in her room." Then Ed growled, "Behave yourself, Amir. I'm warning you."

Amir looked shocked. He and Ed had gotten along well over the years, but Ed's tone and facial expression made Amir pause. *Have I done something to upset him?*

Amir nodded to Ed and entered the house.

"Natalie?" he called from the front room. "It's me."

"Back here," Natalie's voice called back.

Amir stepped around the few boxes remaining on the floor next to the open door and followed her voice. He had been to the house numerous times, but something seemed different—off for some reason. He didn't understand how off it was until he reached Natalie's room... and found it bare except for Natalie sitting on the bed, glaring at him.

"What's up, Buddy?" he demanded. "Why did you leave me in Seoul without saying anything? And why haven't you responded to my calls and texts?"

Natalie stared at him in utter disgust. "You're actually asking that question? You're actually acting like you didn't do anything to make me want to leave you in Korea?" She snorted with disgust. "You're pathetic."

They stared at each other in silence for a moment. Then

Love Lost, Love Found

Natalie looked down and patted the mattress next to her. "Sit here, Amir. We need to talk."

"Sure." He stepped forward. Glancing around, he asked, "Where's your stuff? Are you finally getting your own place?"

Natalie didn't answer. She just shook her head and patted the mattress again, looking annoyed.

Amir thought, *She can't still be pissed about that last prank, can she? She's probably pranking me to get revenge, but if she hid cameras in here, she's better than I am. Everything's gone.* He looked around again, hoping to spot a camera, but he didn't see any.

Amir knelt in front of her. He reached for her hand, but she yanked it back.

"Don't touch me. Sit down and keep your hands to yourself, or leave." She kept her voice steady, but her tone spoke volumes.

Amir complied. *She IS pissed. I'll have to be extra charming to win her back after this one, I guess.*

He reached for her knee, and began, "Look, Natalie, I'm so sorry about—"

Natalie pulled away. "I told you not to touch me, Amir. You're not here to talk, you're here to listen, so just sit there. Don't touch, don't talk, don't do anything."

"Okay," Amir said softly. He pulled back and put his hands in his lap, stunned at how angry Natalie was and how much control she was clearly exerting to keep herself calm. "I'm really sorry. I know I said that, but I am."

Natalie frowned. "Amir, this is my time to talk, not yours, okay? Just listen with your ears, not your mouth."

Amir nodded.

Natalie looked down, then she shifted so she could face him. "What you did… there's no excuse. Because I missed my interview with the U.S. Consulate in Sydney, I lost my chance at that internship. You know how much it meant to me. You know that I need space from you to figure out where we're going and what I want, since I seem to be the only one of us who is actually thinking about a future together that involves things other than silly, stupid videos. I know you didn't want me to go, to be away from you, to be out of your control, but for you to do what you did to me for your personal… satisfaction, for your control over me, is absolutely unforgivable. Nothing you say or do will change that. Nothing you say or do can fix this. It's the worst thing you've ever done to me, and since you've been escalating your so-called pranks for years, I can… I can barely imagine what you have in store for me in the future. Well, I don't plan to stick around and find out. I'm tired of living my life… walking into a room and wondering where the cameras are, in case I'm the butt of another one of your stupid, childish pranks."

"What are you saying?" Amir asked. *Good God, did I really go too far this time? Is this real and not just for a revenge video?*

"I… can't… I can't do this anymore. It's… it's over, Amir. I'm breaking up with you. And before you start thinking that I'm recording this for a video, look around. There are no cameras in here. This isn't a prank. This is real."

Amir reached for Natalie's arm.

Natalie jerked back and raised her hand to signal Amir to stop. "Don't touch me! I told you not to, and I meant it. Do that again, and I'll have Ed come in here and throw you out. Do you understand?"

"Yes. I'm sorry." Amir withdrew his hand. *I can't let her do this.*

"We're done, Amir. Over. This relationship is… it's no more. You destroyed it. I *loved* you. I wanted to live with you. I wanted to marry you and start a family. Now I can't stand the sight of you. We're through, and you can forget about ever getting me back. I see the real you, now. I see the way you've been manipulating me, the way you've… you've been… emotionally abusing me. For years, Amir. It's the same cycle over and over and over. You take things too far, you rip my heart

Love Lost, Love Found

out, and then you see that you went too far and you apologize. You swear you'll never do it again, you shower me with gifts until I forgive you and take you back, and then, after you feel self-assured again, you do something even more horrible than the last time. And like a *fool*, I keep letting you treat me like a prop in your stupid, stupid videos. Well, I'm not your *prop*, I'm not your *accessory* like you wanted me to be in Seoul, and I'm not your girlfriend. Not anymore. I am my own person, and I'm going to have *nothing* more to do with you. I'll never let you abuse me or disrespect me or treat me like you've treated me ever again. Do you understand, Amir?"

"Natalie…"

"No, Amir, I can't… I can't."

"Natalie…"

"No, Amir, this isn't me asking you, this is me telling you. This isn't a discussion about whether we should break up. We are broken up. It's done. Forever. Don't you get that? I will *never* let you or anyone else ever treat me the way you've treated me, thinking it's okay to mess with my life for your enjoyment or some… power trip. I don't love you anymore, Amir, I don't want to be with you, I don't want to see you, I don't want to know you. You're no longer my boyfriend. You have taken every fond feeling I ever had for you and stomped them into the dust. I… I feel nothing for you, Amir. Nothing. It's like you're dead to me right now, and that'll never change. It's. Over."

Amir assumed his "weepy" face, which was the first step in the cycle that had always worked to get Natalie to forgive him. "I'm sorry, Natalie, I'm sorry. I didn't realize… I know I messed up… I didn't think. It was just a stupid prank… a joke. I didn't think it through. I was an idiot—"

"How could any rational person think that what you did could be a funny thing to do to someone? To someone you claim to love? What could possibly be funny about causing me to miss an interview so I'd lose a job? This wasn't about being funny, this is about you trying to control me, and I'm tired of it. It's not funny, it's rude... evil. It's not what a lover does, it's what a snake does, and you know what you do with snakes around here, Amir? You don't laugh, you cut their heads off. Well, I'm not going to cut *your* head off, but I am going to cut you out of my life, just like you'd cut out a cancer, because that's all you are... a cancer, eating away at my soul. Well, no more."

Amir was now completely convinced that Natalie was not revenge pranking him. *She's serious this time. This is real. No! I can't let her do this. I won't allow it! My video channel will fail without her! She's the reason people watch it.*

"I'm an idiot..."

"Yes, you are, Amir. How could you do that to me? It's clear you don't love me, you never loved me. If you did, you wouldn't wait for me to initiate everything between us. I was the one who first said, 'I love you.' I was the one who first said I wanted us to do the naughty. I was the one who first said I wanted us to live together. We've been together for four years, Amir, and we still don't live together. We still aren't engaged. Why? Because you don't really love me. You love the *idea* of me. You love embarrassing me in your stupid videos for the world to see, for my family and friends to see. You humiliate me in public *for entertainment*, and you call that love? What a crock! And you expect me to just take that and keep on loving you? No, Amir. That's not happening. Have you ever read the comments to the videos you post that show how you treat me? Nearly everyone asks why I put up with it, with you. And you know, I finally had to admit that they're right. I no longer have to put up with it... or you. I'm tired of making excuses for you, I'm tired of letting you do this to me again and again and again. I'm tired of being abused, of being controlled, of being humiliated, and of being in a loveless relationship with a man-boy who will never grow up and will never treat me the way I deserve to be treated. I don't want your money, and I don't want gifts from you. I want respect, I want love, and you're obviously incapable of giving that. No, Amir, there's no love left in me for you. You destroyed the last of it when you caused me to miss my interview and lose the job offer. Well, I'm not sticking around so you can do it to me again. I'm not just breaking up with you; I'm leaving."

Amir was shocked. "What do you mean you're leaving?"

"I'm leaving Brisbane. In fact, I'm leaving Queensland."

"And going where?" Amir demanded.

"That's none of your business." Natalie said defiantly.

"You can't do that. I won't let you go." Amir aggressively grabbed for Natalie's arm.

Natalie slapped his arm away from her and kept her hand up to slap him across the face if he moved toward her again. "You can't stop me, Amir. You don't own me, and you no longer control me. I'm going, and that's that."

"You don't have to leave, Natalie," Amir protested, trying to look weepy again. "I'm sorry, and I swear... I *swear* I'll never do it again. I'll take down the video channel. No more pranks, no more videos."

Natalie snorted. "Words, Amir. Just more words you don't mean and promises you won't keep." She gestured to the boxes against the wall. "Your words mean nothing to me, and neither do your gifts. Those boxes contain everything you ever bought me as a bribe to forgive you for pranking me... everything except for my car, which I'm keeping because you destroyed my old one. Oh, I'm keeping some of the clothes you bought me on our travels, but everything else you bought is in those boxes. Take them with you and do what you want to with them. If you leave them here, Ed will burn them, like I did earlier to all of your photos."

"What?"

"Yes, I burned all your photos... and I deleted the ones on my phone and on my social media accounts. All of my online friends and followers know we're broken up already, and they know why. I don't want to see your face anymore, Amir. I don't want to be reminded of someone who treats me like crap all the time. You clearly don't love me, and you never did."

"I'm sorry—"

"God, stop *apologizing*, Amir. Words... I've heard them all before, and I don't believe them because you've never meant them all the other times you've said them. I'm just done... done with you, done with this, done with it all. Your words mean nothing to me. I'm sick and tired of putting up with you."

"Natalie, please, can't we talk about this? I love you. You're the most important person in the world to me."

"Why? Because you get more internet likes when you post videos of you abusing me? That's not love, that's ego. It's over, Amir. Accept it."

Amir tried to grab her by the shoulders, but Natalie stood up from the bed and backed away. "I told you not to touch me. It's time for me to go. You need to leave. I don't want to see you ever again, I don't want to hear from you ever again, I don't want to know you anymore."

Amir tried to block her, but Ed stepped into the room and shoved Amir back onto the bed. "She said not to touch her, Amir. If you won't listen to her, by God you'll listen to me."

Amir glared at Ed. If Ed weren't bigger and stronger, Amir would have fought him to get to Natalie, but Amir knew this was a fight he couldn't win.

Ed looked at Natalie. "Go ahead and leave, Sis. I'll make sure he doesn't follow you."

Natalie nodded. "Make sure he takes those boxes." She took Amir's key from her pocket and tossed it onto the bed next to him.

Ed looked at the boxes filled with Amir's things. "I will. Call me when you get there."

Natalie gave Ed a kiss on the cheek. She looked down at

Love Lost, Love Found

Amir, still on the bed, and just shook her head.

Amir panicked. "Natalie, stop! You're my soulmate. You can't leave me. I'll never let you go! We're supposed to be together forever!"

Natalie left the bedroom. As she walked to the front door, she heard Amir shout, "Don't leave me!"

She exited the house, took off her sandals and changed into a pair of runners (sneakers), and got into her car to start the ten-hour drive to Sydney.

CHAPTER 1

Pelham Campbell sat in his Bethesda, Maryland office, tying up loose ends before his trip to Australia. He preferred to be called "Pelham" to distinguish himself from all of the other Jamiesons, Jameses, and Jamies in his family. At thirty-three, the ruggedly handsome advertising executive was often mistaken for being a rancher. In fact, he was one of the more successful advertising partners in the United States. His sandy-brown hair, close-cropped beard, piercing hazel eyes, warm smile, sincere and friendly manner, and athletic build made him one of the more popular and eligible bachelors in the greater Washington D.C. metropolitan area, but no one had yet managed to win his heart.

Pelham glanced at the photos and certificates on his walls, which reminded him of his days working in one of the larger advertising agencies on Madison Avenue in New York. In the center of the photos was one of him shaking hands with Wes Mason, his mentor at the Madison Avenue agency and now the senior partner at Mason, Campbell, Alvarado, & Jürgen, LLP—the firm that Pelham and Wes had started a few years earlier. The firm's mission was to provide Madison Avenue quality ads and services to smaller clients who couldn't afford top-tier prices, but still needed top-tier-styled campaigns and branding services to advance their business. Wes managed the firm's headquarters in Pittsburgh, but the three other partners each controlled different territories around the country: Pelham in the Mid-Atlantic and Southeast, Bridget Alvarado in the Southwest, and Phillip Jürgen in the Northwest. Wes' staff handled the Midwest and Northeast. While Wes and the other two partners were mostly involved in advertising and brand management, Pelham also provided all training workshops and seminars world-wide on brand-management and publicity services for smaller clients—businesses and individuals. That was what the upcoming trip to Australia was for—to conduct a number of workshops and seminars in Sydney to help people understand what brand management and publicity was for, and to prove that it could be done affordably, regardless of the size of the client.

A knock on Pelham's office door startled him. He looked up and saw Lauren O'Donovan, his Office Manager, standing in his doorway. Pelham smiled. "Yes, Lauren?"

"Sorry to intrude on your thoughts, Boss," she said pleasantly. "Wes is on line three for you."

"Thanks!"

Pelham reached for the phone and pressed line three. "What's up, Wes?"

"Hi, Pelham. Just wanted to check in and see if you're ready for your month in Australia."

"Apart from having to spend two days traveling there and two days traveling back, I think I'm all set. Any last-minute instructions?"

"Yes," Wes replied. "You remember the intern assessment I asked you to handle while you're there?"

"Yeeees," Pelham answered slowly. "Something about the candidate missing her Consulate interview and you rescinding her internship offer, right?"

"Right. The candidate's name is Natalie Patterson. She used to live in Brisbane, but she lives in Sydney now. She has had her Consulate interview, and the paperwork is making its way through State Department channels. I hope to hear back in the next few weeks if her visa has been granted. But we need to make certain whether missing that initial Consulate interview was an unfortunate event or indicative of a character flaw that should disqualify her from the program. I need you to assess that and let me know your opinion."

"How do you want me to do that?" Pelham asked.

"Find out why she missed the Consulate interview, and then put her through a real-world evaluation," Wes stated. "She's signed up for your first workshop. Let her learn the basics. Then have her assist you with the remaining workshops, seminars, and lectures. See how she does. If you think she's up to it, give her a bigger role in each subsequent event. If she handles the responsibility, that's a good sign. If she wilts under the pressure... well, we'll have our answer."

"Got it. Let's say that she handles the responsibility, and my overall assessment of her is positive. What then?"

"That depends on when and if her visa gets approved. If it gets approved while you're there, bring her back with you and use her for your sessions in New York, Orlando, and Chicago next month. You're always saying that you need a second person to help out. Perhaps she could fill that role."

"And if her visa doesn't get approved in time?" Pelham asked.

"We'll deal with that when the time comes," Wes replied.

"Do you know where she'll be assigned once she gets here? Assuming everything goes well, of course."

Wes paused for a moment. "Since you're doing the assessment, you get dibs. If you want her in your office, she's yours. If not, we'll assign her to one of the other offices."

"Fair enough. How do I contact her?"

"She'll find you during the workshop she's attending."

"And how will we handle having her working with me for the three weeks after that?" Pelham asked. "I doubt she'd be willing to do all that for free."

Wes chuckled. "Good point. We'll offer her the standard internship hourly rate for her time. Have her complete and sign a weekly timecard, and Accounting will wire the cash to you to pay her with. I don't want to show her as an employee until your assessment is completed, but she should receive compensation for her time and effort. Cash should work well."

"Right. Who's going to tell her that she has to commit a month to us before even finding out whether or not she's getting the internship?"

Wes laughed. "I'll see to it that she knows before you arrive. Satisfied?"

"Satisfied."

"Good. Safe travels, my friend, and keep in touch, okay?"

"Okay."

Wes ended the call.

Pelham smiled and started re-verifying all the materials he was taking to Australia so nothing was forgotten or overlooked.

Natalie re-read the email from Mason, Campbell, Alvarado, & Jürgen, LLP. *A whole month? I was thrilled when they told me I could attend the seminar next week for free, in return for being available to meet with this J. Pelham Campbell bloke, but now I'll be working with him for the three weeks after that as part of my candidate assessment? Well, getting the time off work is no problem, since Aunt Rachel is my boss. And they ARE offering to pay me for my time. If this is the price for getting a second chance after what Amir did to me, then I guess it's worth it.*

She read the email one more time before going to find her

aunt and explaining why she wouldn't be at work for the next four weeks.

As she passed one of the front windows in Aunt Rachel's house, she glanced out and saw a familiar figure across the street. *What the hell! What is Amir doing out there?*

Natalie moved back away from the window, watching him stare at the house. *How does he even know I'm here?*

This was not the first time that she had seen Amir watching her since she moved to Sydney two months earlier, but this was the first time he had shown up at Aunt Rachel's house. *He has got to stop this, but I'm not going out there to confront him.*

Natalie went to find Aunt Rachel to tell her that she needed four weeks off from work, but said nothing about Amir being across the street. When Aunt Rachel agreed, Natalie went back to her room to send a reply to the Internship Coordinator at Mason, Campbell, Alvarado, & Jürgen, LLP, confirming that she'd be available for the month. As she passed the front windows, she noticed that Amir was no longer visible. *Where has he gone?*

Pelham's plane landed at Sydney Kingsford Smith International Airport the following Sunday. He caught a cab to the Sydney Hilton on George Street, where he had a suite reserved and where the first two weeks of workshops were being held.

After checking in, he reviewed the meeting-room set up—which consisted of nine round tables seating five participants each, a large screen in the front of the room, and a table and lectern near the screen for Pelham to use—and then he dropped off his bags in his suite before exploring the rest of the hotel. After that, he returned to his suite, unpacked, ordered dinner from room service, and started preparing for the workshop the next morning.

He arrived at the meeting-room an hour before the workshop was scheduled to begin. As he approached the doors to the room, he saw a woman across the lobby who seemed to be looking for someone. She was tall, even in the flat sandals she was wearing, and she wore a short, red print dress that showed off her long, lean legs. A sweater seemed to be her only concession to the chilly temperatures outside—lows in the low 50s and highs in the mid-60s. The outfit and her long, straight hair, suggested that she was young, but even from a distance, Pelham thought she was stunning. In one hand she carried a notebook, and in her other hand she carried her phone.

Pelham entered the meeting-room and began attaching his laptop to the projector provided by the hotel. The first workshop slide soon appeared on the screen in the front of the room. Satisfied, Pelham grabbed the handouts for the first day from his roller-case. As he turned to place them on the tables around the room, he saw the young woman standing in the doorway.

"Excuse me," she said pleasantly. "Are you Mr. Campbell?"

"Call me Pelham," he said, distributing the handouts around the room. "Are you here for the workshop?"

She entered the room and nodded. "I'm Natalie Patterson. I'm the internship candidate you're supposed to be meeting with this week."

Pelham smiled and put down the stack of handouts. Walking toward her, he held out his hand. "Welcome, Natalie! Did you receive an email about what's happening for the next four weeks?"

She shook his hand and nodded. "Yes. I'm to attend the workshop this week, and then I'm to help you conduct your remaining workshops and seminars while you're in Sydney.

Somewhere in all of that, I'm supposed to make time for you to assess me as a candidate for the internship program."

Pelham nodded. "That's right. Are you okay with that arrangement? You'll be paid for your time, you know."

Natalie flashed a smile. "That was in the email I was sent. I'm okay with the arrangements. I want this internship, and if this is what I have to do to get it, then I'm good with that."

Pelham cocked his head to one side. "Why do you want the internship so badly? If you don't mind me asking."

"I studied international business and international marketing at university," Natalie replied. "But to put my degree into practice, I need to work outside Australia. I also have experience in branding, so your firm's emphasis on brand management and publicity intrigued me. I love to travel, and I've always wanted to work abroad. After researching your firm and the internship program, it seemed like a great way to learn and possibly earn the chance to live and work in America."

Pelham looked at her. He was an excellent judge of character, which was necessary in his business. She seemed sincere, but he could tell she was holding something back. "That's not the only reason, is it?"

Natalie blinked, and her smile faded somewhat. "No, it isn't. I'll be happy to tell you the rest of my reasons, but..." she looked around and then back at Pelham... "this might not be the best time or place for *that* conversation."

Pelham smiled and nodded. "No worries. We'll have plenty of time to discuss that over the next several weeks."

Natalie's smile returned. "Thank you. Where do you want me to sit?"

Pelham gestured around the empty room. "Pick any place you like. There are no assigned seats."

Natalie nodded and placed her notebook on the center table, in front of the seat facing the screen and the lectern. "Do you need any help passing those around?" she asked, pointing to the stack of handouts Pelham had set down when she entered the meeting-room.

Pelham nodded. "Yes, thank you."

Natalie picked up the stack and finished placing them around the room. Pelham went back to the lectern to complete his preparations for the opening session.

Pelham watched her placing the handouts at each table. *This is the girl I'm supposed to assess for the internship? She's gorgeous! How am I supposed to concentrate on my work while I'm here if I have to look at her all day? I'll be distracted all the time. This is going to take more discipline than I've ever had to muster before. Wes should have warned me.*

Natalie took her seat and watched Pelham prepare for the workshop. She admired his physique, and as she watched him greet the other participants when they arrived, she appreciated the way he immediately put people at ease.

For an older guy, he's not bad looking. After Amir, I wouldn't mind being with someone older who knows how to treat a woman and actually acts like a man, rather than a man-boy. I wonder what his story is. Is he married? I don't see a ring, but some blokes don't wear them. He is single? Divorced? Is he in a relationship? Is he straight? Gay? Undecided? What kind of girl is his type? Would he even go for someone my age? Does his company have rules about co-workers dating? She watched him close the door at the back of the meeting-room. *I guess I'll find out over the next few weeks.*

Natalie shook her head to clear her thoughts when Pelham let all forty-five attendees know that the workshop was about to begin. He started by asking the participants to introduce themselves. Once the introductions were completed, he pushed a button on his laptop to start a video clip on the screen at the front of the room. It was the funniest thing Natalie had ever seen.

The clip was clearly an old advertisement for an appliance retailer. Standing inside a clothes washing machine was a young girl dressed as a cheerleader. The girl twisted from side to side and then started doing the squats to demonstrate that the agitator worked multiple ways. Natalie and the others laughed at how absurd the advertisement was.

The next clip was for the same washing machine, but this advertisement was produced by the manufacturer. It was polished, professional, and left everyone in the room with a completely different impression of the machine and what it could do. No one laughed when the second video clip finished.

"As you can guess, the first clip was made for a small local appliance store in America. It's low budget, the voiceover was the cheerleader's father who owned the store, and it should come as no surprise that his business closed many years ago, since almost all of his advertisements were similar to this."

Pelham paused for a moment before continuing. "The second clip was produced by a major advertising agency for the manufacturer. It's high budget, high quality, and it gets the point across much more effectively than watching a cheerleader buggering around inside the machine."

There were chuckles around the room.

"In the past, this was typical of advertisements shown on television. National retailers and manufacturers produced great advertisements, while local companies produced... well... this." Pelham showed the first clip again, but this time with the sound turned off.

"But what if local companies could produce high quality advertisements within their budgets? Today, you don't need an entire production crew to film an advertisement. A single person with a good cell phone camera, a ring light, and a microphone can create theatre-quality movies, so why not low-cost, high-quality advertisements? For the first time, technology is giving

Love Lost, Love Found

us a whole new way to put the same advertising capabilities—traditionally reserved for major businesses—into the hands of small businesses and individuals. Why aren't we taking advantage of that? Because no one is showing people how to adapt the big budget productions for low budget clients, while preserving the quality and the polish of the advertisements. Well, that's what we're going to talk about this week during this workshop: bringing the quality and brand power that were formerly the exclusive domain of big companies, and adapting them for small companies and even individuals who are working to build and expand upon their brand. Sound good?"

All heads in the room nodded.

"Then let's get started."

When Pelham called an end to the first day's session, Natalie was surprised. The day went by so quickly that she didn't realize it was after five in the afternoon. Between Pelham's examples and insights into the workshop topics, and the lively interactions he had with the other participants, she had learned more about brand management in that first day than during her entire time at university.

As the other attendees exited the room, she stayed behind. "Do you need any help setting up for tomorrow?" she asked.

Pelham smiled. "I will tomorrow morning, but not tonight, thanks."

Natalie nodded. "Do you have plans for dinner?"

Pelham shook his head. "I figured I'd order room service and review my notes for tomorrow. Why? Did you have something in mind?"

"I thought you might want to start your assessment of me," Natalie said. "But if you'd rather do that another time, that's fine, too."

Pelham stared at her for a moment. Then he said, "We can start the assessment tonight, if you want. We can talk while we eat. Any suggestions on a place?"

Natalie shook her head. "I don't get to this part of the city that often, so I don't know what's around here."

"The hotel has a good restaurant. Why don't we eat here?"

Natalie smiled and nodded.

Pelham finished packing up his laptop and notes. "Let me drop these off in my room, and then I'll meet you in the lobby. Okay?"

"Okay." Natalie headed for the escalator downstairs and Pelham headed for the elevators. When she reached the escalator, she saw Pelham standing in front of an elevator—waiting. Then the elevator doors opened, and Pelham disappeared inside.

That is one seriously handsome man, she thought as she rode down to the lobby.

The hotel restaurant wasn't busy that night, so Pelham and Natalie were able to get a table in the far corner of the dining room, where they wouldn't be disturbed.

After they had ordered their meal, Natalie told Pelham about her time in university. Pelham listened until she was finished.

"Impressive grades," he commented when she showed him her transcript. "You mentioned you had experience with branding. Tell me more about that."

Natalie told Pelham about how she had helped Amir with branding his social media video channel.

"What kind of videos are we talking about?" Pelham asked.

"Mostly pranks with hidden cameras to capture reactions," Natalie admitted. "In hindsight, it all seems kind of childish, but part of it was fun at the time."

Love Lost, Love Found

"How do you mean?"

"Well, in the beginning, the pranks were harmless and funny. He and I would prank his friends, so we were a team. But once we had been dating for a while, he started pranking me. Some were funny, some were stupid, but some were... deplorable. The things he did to get a rise out of me for his fans were just plain rude and... emotionally... abusive. That's why we parted ways. I'm over him, but it's clear he's not over me."

"How so?"

"I've caught him following me ever since I left Brisbane. Just the other day, he was standing in front of my aunt's house where I'm staying, and I never told him where she lives. I'll see him waiting outside pubs and theatres, outside my work, or standing on street corners waiting for me to drive by. You know, he's the reason I missed my Consulate appointment."

"How so?" Pelham asked.

"He didn't want me to get the internship, but he did want me to go with him to Seoul for a video content creator's conference. He hacked my phone's calendar, showed us going to Korea the week of the appointment, and moved the Consulate appointment to the next week. I was in Korea when the Consulate and your firm notified me about missing my appointment and losing the internship offer. I flew back to Brisbane that night without telling Amir. You have no idea what I had to do to get the Consulate appointment rescheduled and get your firm to reconsider me as a candidate. It was a nightmare."

"But you were able to meet with the Consulate, and you *are* being considered for the internship," Pelham pointed out.

"Too right, but you're having to assess me as a candidate now before any offers can be made," Natalie responded. "All this because of a stupid, childish prank played on me by a narcissistic man-boy who is more concerned about his fans than he is about my life and what I want."

Pelham leaned back. "Are the videos still out on the

internet?"

Natalie nodded.

"Do you have any objection to me watching them?"

Natalie's face turned red. "If you'd like." She gave him the website address. "Just don't hold them against me. I was in love when I made them. I was a fool, but that's been corrected."

"You said he's following you around Sydney," Pelham commented. "How does he know where you are?"

"I don't know, but I'm starting to have nightmares about it. I see him everywhere each time I close my eyes."

"You said he knows how to access your phone, right?"

Natalie nodded.

"Could he have installed a tracking app on your phone?"

Natalie stared at Pelham, wide-eyed. "How would I know?"

Pelham asked her to take out her phone, and he walked her through the procedure for identifying tracking apps. Two were installed on her phone.

"Crap!" Natalie exclaimed. "How do I get these things off of here?"

Pelham showed her how to remove them. A few minutes later, her phone was free of tracking software.

"What kind of phone does Amir have?" Pelham asked.

Natalie told him the brand.

"You know, that company makes GPS tags that their phone apps can track. I wonder if he planted any of those on you."

Natalie's eyes went wide again. "How do I find them?"

Pelham accessed an app on his phone and showed it to her. "Download this app on your phone, and it will tell you if a tracking tag is operating near you. You should check your purse, your car, your luggage… anything that you've had with you when you were with him. If he's this obsessed with you, there's no telling what he's using to know where you are at all times."

Natalie installed the app and activated it. Confused by what she saw, she showed her phone to Pelham. "What does this mean?"

Pelham looked at the app. "It means that there's an active tracker nearby. Check your purse."

Natalie grabbed her purse, which was a small shoulder bag. She searched it, and then she emptied it so she could search more thoroughly. She didn't see anything, but she felt something inside one of the interior pockets. She reached in and pulled out a flat, square piece of plastic that had the logo of Amir's phone manufacturer on it. "What's this?"

Pelham looked at it. "That's a GPS tag. Anytime you carry that purse, he knows where you are."

Natalie looked panicked. A bus boy walked by the table, carrying a load of dirty dishes. Natalie tossed the tracker into the plastic bin holding the dishes.

Pelham chuckled. "Give it a minute, and then check for any more trackers nearby."

Natalie waited, and then she refreshed the app. "It's not picking anything up," she said.

"Good. Remember to check your car and everything at home. If you find more tags, drop them off all over the city. That way, he'll never know where you are, and he'll be chasing ghosts for weeks."

Natalie laughed as she put her things back into her purse. "Thanks, Pelham." She looked at him with a grin. "What kind of name is Pelham, by the way?"

"It's my middle name," Pelham replied. "My first name is Jamieson, but every male in my family is named Jamieson, James, or Jamie. There are so many of us that my great aunt started numbering us. I didn't want to be known by a number, so I started going by Pelham, just to shake things up."

"So, you're from a big family?" Natalie asked.

"I… was."

The waiter brought their food and placed it on the table. When he left, Natalie said, "I'm sorry."

Pelham nodded. "I still have cousins in the area, but my parents and my sister were killed in a car accident right before Wes Mason and I started the firm. My parents had just finished building their dream house in Bethesda, Maryland—just north of the Potomac River—when the accident occurred. I decided to move into it, rather than sell it. That's why Wes gave me the mid-Atlantic and southeast region. He knew it would allow me to live in Maryland, and he knew the work would help take my mind off of suddenly finding myself an orphan."

They ate in silence for a few minutes. Then Pelham asked, "What about your family?"

Natalie told him about her parents, her brother, her father's Irish roots, and her aunt.

"What do they think about the possibility of you moving to America?"

"They're sad, but they're happy for me," Natalie said. "They always knew that I'd leave Brisbane someday, but as long as we video chat often, and I come back here or they come to see me, then they seem okay with me leaving the country. They want what's best for me, and being away from Australia right now is what's best."

"Because of Amir, or because of the job?" Pelham asked.

"Both," Natalie replied. "The job opportunity is amazing—too good to pass up. The job being in America has its own advantages, and yes, Amir is now a contributing factor. But he's not the only one. I wanted the internship when he and I were still together and doing okay, so he's not the reason I want to go to America, but he's certainly making the idea much sweeter."

"I understand that."

They finished their meal. Once Pelham paid the check, he walked her to her car, which was in the parking deck adjacent to the hotel, near the hotel's loading docks. When they reached her car, Natalie checked for trackers and found two: one inside the bumper and one inside the glovebox.

Love Lost, Love Found

"He's a persistent bugger, isn't he?" Pelham asked as he placed the two trackers on two delivery trucks parked at the loading dock.

"Too right he is, but moving the trackers should keep him occupied and away from me for a while."

They scanned her car again and found no other trackers.

"Same time tomorrow?" she asked, getting into her car.

"See you then," Pelham said. He watched her drive off, and then headed back into the hotel.

As he rode up the elevator, he thought, *I think I'll watch some of those videos tonight. It'll help me see what kind of branding she was doing, it'll give me insights into her sense of humor, and it will help me understand the dynamic with Amir, which should provide a clearer picture of her character.*

Chapter 2

Natalie was waiting for Pelham when he arrived at the meeting-room the next morning. Pelham noticed that she was dressed more appropriately for the weather—black skinny jeans, laced ankle boots, and a sweater. The jeans still showed off her amazing legs, but Pelham thought that they wouldn't be as distracting as the short dress she wore the day before.

"Good morning, Pelham," she said pleasantly.

"Good morning, Natalie. How was your evening?"

Natalie beamed. "It was busy, but perfect. I found eleven more trackers in my stuff, and now they're all moving about the city inside delivery trucks, on motorcycles, and even inside the bumper of a police car."

Pelham laughed.

"I'll keep sweeping my car and my stuff daily, but this should keep Amir completely baffled about what's going on for weeks," Natalie added with a mischievous twinkle in her eye.

Pelham hooked his laptop to the projector. Natalie put her notebook down at the same spot as the previous day, and then she grabbed the handouts and started distributing them around the tables.

"I watched several of your videos last night," Pelham said.

Natalie froze for a moment, and then she continued placing the handouts around the room. "What did you think?"

"I now understand what you mean about how Amir and the pranks changed over time," Pelham replied. "Some of the early pranks were clever and in good fun, but once Amir started getting his prank ideas from his fans, who clearly didn't have *your* best interests in mind, the pranks became twisted and... well... evil. I can't believe some of what he pulled. In my opinion, that's not how you treat someone you proclaim to love. Ever. Frankly, I'm amazed you stayed with him so long."

"He was a good manipulator," Natalie responded. "He made his antics seem normal, and my reaction to them seem abnormal, like the problem was with me. And then he'd buy my affection so I'd be distracted and wouldn't see what was really happening. It wasn't until the Korea trip that I woke up and saw our relationship for what it really was—a joke. I was his prop, an accessory to make his fans happy. I figure the reason he's stalking me is because his fans are furious that I left, and now he has to get me back to make them happy again."

"Any chance of that happening?" Pelham asked.

"None," Natalie stated. "I won't even give him the chance to try to convince me to come back. Once it's over, it's over. There's no going back now."

Pelham nodded. "He certainly appeared affectionate in several of the videos."

"Yeah, because he was getting what he wanted. You probably saw how he behaved when things didn't go right or when I pranked him."

Pelham nodded. "He could dish it out, but he couldn't take it. I watched several videos of him getting loud, trying to take the camera away from you, and storming about like an oversized, spoiled child."

"That's exactly right," Natalie agreed. "He'd get scary to

make me back down, and when I wouldn't, he'd get weepy to manipulate me into forgiving his behavior. After that, he'd buy me expensive gifts, so I'd forget all about what he'd done. It was a pattern, but it took me years to see it."

"It's hard to see the patterns from the inside," Pelham noted. "Sometimes you have to be on the outside looking in to see them."

"And that's what happened when I flew home from Seoul." Natalie said. "Once I was away from him, I could see everything clearly. And once seen, it couldn't be unseen."

Pelham nodded. "Well, I think it shows great strength of character to walk away from something that toxic after you invested four years into what was clearly a one-sided relationship."

Natalie smiled. "Thank you for that. Part of me is still ashamed it took me so long. The abuse had become normal. I should never have let him start it in the first place."

Pelham held up his hand. "Don't look at it that way. Manipulators will always find a way in. Just be grateful that you finally saw it for what it was and walked away. Imagine if the two of you had gotten married or started a family before you recognized what was going on. You're one of the fortunate ones. You saw it while there was still time to get clear of the situation."

Natalie nodded and sat down. "So, you don't hold what I let happen against me?"

"Not at all," Pelham assured her. "And I could see immediately how you improved the branding on his channel. I might call on you during today's session to talk a bit about that. Feel up to it?"

Natalie's eyes went wide and her face lit up. "Actually?"

Pelham nodded.

"I'd love that!"

Love Lost, Love Found

Pelham and Natalie had dinner again that night. The front desk had recommended a nearby restaurant that was within walking distance, and in spite of the chilly night air, it was a pleasant walk and enjoyable company for them both.

After they ordered their meals, Pelham asked questions to assess what Natalie had learned about branding and publicity from university and from her time with Amir. Even though most of her experience came from branding via social media, Pelham was impressed with her understanding of the subject and her thoughts on adapting social media branding to other advertising platforms.

"Your grasp of the concepts is refreshing, since so few universities seem to emphasize the practical aspects of the work these days," Pelham said after their food arrived. "The internship will build on that and give you real-world experience taking those concepts and using them to create advertising campaigns and publicity events. But do you know what the most important part of working with clients on campaigns and events is?"

Natalie, who was about to take a bite of her dinner, froze with her fork halfway between the plate and her mouth. "I... I'm not sure."

"Problem solving," Pelham answered. "The real work performed by an advertising agency or marketing firm is helping the client solve a problem. How we structure the campaign, the events we coordinate, are all focused on solving problems, so first we need to understand the problem that needs to be solved, what the client wants the result to be, and then tailor our services to achieve those results. In the social media world, the results are more straightforward: more views, more likes, and more shares, hopefully leading to better monetization. In the business world, it's about increasing the number of customers, increasing sales, funding research-and-development on new or better products, expanding into new markets, and launching new product lines. Same concepts, different scale."

Natalie nodded. "And do you think I'm ready for the business world?"

Pelham looked at her intently. Then he said, "If I had to give my assessment today, I'd say yes. I think you have the skills and talents. What you need, and what the internship provides, is experience applying those skills and talents in ways that are different from what you're used to."

As they continued eating, Natalie asked, "So, what happens next week?"

"We have another workshop that starts on Monday. Then the last two weeks will be a series of lectures, seminars, and mini-workshops at two universities."

"What are you going to do on the weekends?"

Pelham put his fork down. "I usually explore the cities where I'm working or find some other diversion to keep me busy," he said. "Why? What are you going to be doing?"

"I thought you might like someone to show you around." Natalie smiled as she tucked her hair behind her right ear. "Ordinarily, I'd suggest heading to Bondi Beach to swim and get some sun, but it's going to be too chilly for that. There are other sites around the city worth seeing, though."

Pelham felt his heart start to beat faster as he looked at Natalie's smile. He took a bite and chewed slowly, giving him time to think. *It would be good to have someone show me around so I don't get lost, but I have to be careful. She's a candidate for an internship, and she's ten years younger than I am. I'm a partner in my firm. I can't do anything that could be seen as placing personal conditions on a job offer or taking advantage of a much younger person, although given her free and easy demeanor, I imagine she's more experienced with men than I am with women. She's from a different culture than I am, and what passes as okay here is probably quite different from what passes for okay back home. At the same time, I don't want to send wrong or mixed messages that could damage our working relationship while I'm here... or once we're in America, if she gets the internship.* He swallowed his bite. *As long as I keep things professional and friendly, but not too friendly, I should be fine.*

Pelham nodded. "That sounds like fun. It's always good to be with someone who knows the area."

Natalie smiled, and for a moment, Pelham got lost in her eyes and her smile. *Discipline, Pelham old man. Discipline. Remember the rules.*

Pelham took another bite. *Stupid rules.*

The rest of the first workshop went well. After the first time Pelham called on Natalie to relate some of her social media branding experiences, she felt more confident participating in the discussions.

Pelham and Natalie had dinner each night that week, walking to a different nearby restaurant recommended by the hotel concierge. They never did anything together after dinner, but Pelham was beginning to wonder if Natalie wanted them to be spending more time together. *Plenty of time to explore that this weekend.*

Before they parted on Friday evening, they made arrangements for Natalie to meet Pelham for breakfast the next morning before going sightseeing. As Pelham walked her to her car, she said, "I've been scanning everything every day like you taught me, and no more trackers. I haven't seen Amir any this week, so he's either chasing the other trackers or he's staying in Brisbane for a while."

She scanned her car, but no trackers were found. Pelham watched her drive off, and then he walked back to the hotel lobby so he could catch the elevator to his floor.

As soon as he entered the room, his cell phone rang. He recognized the number. "Hi, Wes."

"Hi, Pelham. How did the first workshop go?"

"It was great. Good interaction from all the participants."

"And what about our intern candidate?"

"She participated, too. I've completed my initial assessment, if you'd like to hear it. I still want to watch her in action during the next three weeks, but I'm confident in what I've concluded so far."

"Let's hear it."

Pelham sat down on the couch. "Okay. Missing the first Consulate appointment was not a character flaw. In fact, it wasn't her fault at all. Someone she is no longer involved with didn't want her to get the internship, so he sabotaged her by changing her calendar so she thought that the appointment was a week later than scheduled. She ended her relationship with him, and she's clearly willing to do whatever is necessary to be one of our interns. As far as her skills and talents, I'd say she has more than most of our interns, and she has experience applying them, even though it's only with social media, so far. Barring any problems that could arise while she helps me over the next few weeks, I think we should re-offer her a spot in our program."

Wes was silent for a moment. "Are you sure?"

"I am."

"Good. Because I just heard from my contact at the State Department, and her visa has been approved. She has an appointment at the Consulate on Wednesday at ten to finalize everything."

"Can I tell her that the next time I see her?"

"Of course."

Pelham started to end the call, but then he asked, "How come you didn't warn me about what she looks like?"

"How would I know what she looks like?" Wes asked.

Love Lost, Love Found

"Because you were on at least one of the video interviews with her," Pelham reminded him.

"Oh, right. Yeah, she's a looker isn't she?"

"That she is."

"And that didn't affect your assessment of her in any way, right?"

"You know me better than that, Wes."

"Fortunately, I do."

"But since you bring it up, if she gets assigned to my office, what are the rules regarding fraternization? I haven't had an intern before."

"You want to know if you're allowed to see her socially?" Wes sounded more amused than surprised.

"I want to know if it's allowed. And not just for me. Remember, there are men in my office who'd probably jump at the chance to be with her. I need to know how to manage any situation, regardless of whether or not I'm the one involved."

"Hmmm. Well, first of all, as an intern, she'll report to Beverly Houston, the Internship Coordinator. You'll assign and oversee her work, but the Internship Coordinator is her administrative manager. So as long as she's not in your direct chain of command, fraternization is not an issue, although I think you'd agree that it could lead to complications. Now, if she's offered a permanent position at the end of the internship, a romantic relationship with a colleague could cause a problem. She wouldn't be able to report to someone she's involved with. So, if there's a relationship that already exists, or is growing, she'd have to report to a different office. She could still work out of the Maryland office, but she'd have to be administratively managed by someone here at corporate. Does that help?"

"Yes. It's good to know these things up front."

"You're not thinking about getting involved with her, are you?" Wes asked. "I know she's smoking hot, but…"

Pelham hesitated before answering. "I just need to know

where the lines are and what the rules are. Besides, I'm ten years older than she is. To someone her age, that makes me ancient. No, I don't see any chance of something happening between us."

"Okay, Pelham. Just don't let yourself get distracted. I've seen the Sydney ladies before. It's a target rich environment for beauties."

Pelham laughed. "No worries, Wes. I'm here to do a job, not to up my body count."

"Okay. Call me next week and let me know how things are going. And remember, I need your final recommendations on Natalie before your last week down there, so we can make arrangements for her to fly to the States with you."

"You'll have it in plenty of time," Pelham assured him.

Pelham was waiting in the lobby when Natalie arrived the next morning.

"I thought you'd be at the table," she said when she walked up to him.

"Didn't want to start without you," he said, escorting her to the largest of the three restaurants. "Besides, I have something interesting to tell you."

"What is it?" Natalie asked, excitedly.

"After we sit down."

Natalie groaned.

As soon as they were seated at their table, Natalie leaned forward. "What's the news?"

Pelham smiled and opened the menu. "I wonder what's good here. I usually eat at the smaller restaurant."

Natalie started bouncing impatiently. "Tell me, Pelham! What's the news?"

He looked up from his menu. "Oh, that. You have an appointment at ten o'clock on Wednesday morning."

Natalie stared at him. "And?"

"And what?"

"Where's the appointment?" she asked.

"Oh. At the U.S. Consulate."

Natalie looked confused. "Why do I have an appointment at the Consulate?"

Pelham smiled. "Because your visa was granted, and you have to go complete the process so you can legally enter, work, and live in the United States."

Natalie squealed with delight. "Does that mean I'm in the internship program?"

"Let's just say that this is the last hurdle before any offer can be made, but the final offer depends on how things go over the next couple of weeks. However, I talked to Wes last night, and I gave you a glowing recommendation. Barring any problems over the next three weeks, I think you're in."

Without thinking, Natalie launched herself across the table and gave Pelham a hug. Then she realized what she was doing and sat back down. Pelham just smiled as her face turned several shades of red from embarrassment. After she regained her composure, she asked, "So, what happens now?"

"We enjoy our weekend, and we start the next workshop on Monday. I'll coach you on what your role will be between now and then. You'll also have to keep your appointment at the Consulate Wednesday. If all goes well over the next few weeks, you'll fly back to the States with me. The week after I get back to Maryland, I'll be traveling to New York, Orlando, Chicago, and then back to Maryland. You'll be going with me to help, like you'll be doing for the rest of the time I'm here. After that, you'll either be assigned to my office, or you'll be assigned to one of the other regional offices."

"When will that get decided?" Natalie asked.

"Well, it's up to me," Pelham confessed, "and it all depends on how things go here and in the three cities we'll be going to once we leave Australia. In the meantime, you should start getting your affairs in order. You'll need to decide if you want to use a bank here or a bank in the States. You can open an American-based bank account online and wire your money there, but that's your choice. Then you'll need to go through your things and select what you're taking to America. Anything you don't take, you'll want to put in storage or get rid of it. I'd suggest selling your car, but that's up to you, and you'll probably want to get a new cell phone over there that can't be tampered with by you-know-who, but that's also up to you."

Pelham could tell by looking at Natalie's face that the full reality of moving across the world for at least a year was hitting her full force.

"There's so much to do," she said softly.

"And I'm here to help," Pelham said. "We'll get everything done."

Natalie smiled. Then she looked embarrassed again. "Sorry about the hug. I don't know what came over me."

Pelham chuckled. "Don't worry about it. In your position, I probably would have done the same thing."

Natalie beamed, clearly happy that Pelham wasn't going to hold her emotional outburst against her.

Pelham looked down at his menu. *That's the first time I've ever been turned on by a spontaneous act of gratitude. I need to be extra careful over the next three weeks, or I'm going to find myself in real trouble.*

The waiter came by to take their breakfast orders.

"What's the plan for this weekend?" he asked once the waiter had left.

"I thought you might like to do the more touristy things this weekend, and then we can do some of the more interesting things over the next two weekends," Natalie replied.

"Such as?"

"I was thinking that the two most typical places to go today are the Sydney Opera House, which has a one-hour walking tour, and then the Sydney Taronga Zoo. If you're up for it, there's a dinner cruise around the harbor that's quite nice. Tomorrow, I was thinking about seeing the Royal Botanic Gardens in the morning, and a harbor sightseeing cruise in the afternoon, just so you can see everything better than you do at night. That'll leave us time to prepare for the workshop next week."

Pelham nodded. "Good thinking. What about the next two weekends?"

"I thought you'd like to get out of the city," Natalie replied, "so I want to take you on a day trip to the Blue Mountains. There are two tours I really like that we can choose from. If we do that on Saturday, that leaves us Sunday to prepare for the seminars and lectures the next week. For your last weekend in Sydney, there's a day-long wine and distillery tour out at Hunter Valley. Again, we do that on Saturday and spend Sunday getting ready for your, or our, last week here."

The waiter came by and brought coffee and juice.

"What do you think?" Natalie asked once the waiter had left. "There are also bus tours like they have in London if you'd rather do that."

"No, I like your suggestions," Pelham said approvingly. "It all sounds like great ways to spend the weekends."

Natalie beamed. "I'm glad. It seems a shame to just stay in the city your entire time here... even a city as lovely as Sydney."

Pelham nodded. "What time is the Opera House tour?"

Natalie checked her phone. "First tour is at nine, and the second tour is at ten-thirty. The zoo is open from nine to five."

"And what about the dinner cruises?"

Natalie checked her phone. "The four-course dinner leaves at seven-thirty and returns at nine-thirty, and the six-course dinner and wine tasting leaves at seven and returns at ten. They depart from two different docks. The dress code is what they call 'smart casual.'"

"Do you have a preference?" Pelham asked.

"Since we're going to a winery in two weeks, let's do the four-course dinner tonight," Natalie suggested.

"Good idea. That also gives us time to change."

"I brought a change of clothes with me," Natalie said.

"I like that," Pelham noted. "It's always good to be prepared, especially when you're doing the planning."

Natalie's smile, and her beautiful eyes looking at him, made Pelham's heart feel like it had skipped a beat.

Chapter 3

Touring the Opera House was amazing. They arrived in time for the first tour, and were soon walking through the impressive iconic structure.

After the tour, Natalie drove them north across the Sydney Harbour Bridge to the Mosman shoreline, where the zoo was located. Pelham hadn't been to a zoo since he was in high school, and he found the Australian native wildlife fascinating. They ate mostly snacks as they toured each of the exhibits. Natalie pointed out some of the animal species that Pelham might not have seen before, including birds that Pelham never knew existed.

"What does the word 'Taronga' mean?" Pelham asked as they looked at the koalas.

"It's Aborigine for 'beautiful view'," she replied.

As they left the zoo, Natalie asked, "You seemed to enjoy yourself in there. What was your favorite exhibit?"

Pelham looked at her. "I know I'm supposed to say the koalas or the kangaroos, but honestly, it was the sun bears. I've seen bears in the wild before in the States, but there was something about those little guys that I can't explain. They were just… beautiful. What about you? What's your favorite?"

"The koalas," Natalie admitted, grinning. "I can't help it. They're just so cute!"

Pelham glanced at his watch as they walked back to Natalie's car. "Where do we go for the dinner cruise?"

"Circular Quay Wharf, which is not far from your hotel. We should have no problem getting back to the Hilton, getting changed, and making our way to the Wharf in time."

Traffic was light as Natalie drove south over the Sydney Harbour Bridge. They arrived at the hotel, parked the car in the deck, and headed for the hotel lobby. Natalie carried a small bag with her that contained a change of clothes.

As they rode up the elevator, Pelham realized that Natalie would be joining him in his hotel room to change. But they were already in the elevator, so Pelham knew it was too late to make a different suggestion.

When they arrived at his suite, he suggested that she change first, and he showed her where the oversized bathroom was. While she was changing, Pelham selected the clothes he'd be wearing that night. Since the weather was supposed to drop into the low fifties, he decided to wear a coat over his blazer to stay warm.

Natalie emerged from the bathroom a few minutes later. She wore a pair of close-fitting slacks, stylish shoes with heels, and a sweater top. Her hair was pulled back into a high ponytail, and she had touched up her make-up around her eyes and lips. The outfit made her look like she was in her late-twenties, rather than her early-twenties, and the clothes accentuated her amazing figure and long, lean legs.

"All yours," she said, gesturing toward the bathroom door.

"Back in a minute," Pelham said.

He entered the bathroom and closed the door behind him. He stripped off clothes, washed his face, and dressed again quickly. Then he exited the bathroom, hung up clothes, and returned to the living room.

Love Lost, Love Found

Natalie was standing next to the window, gazing out at the view. When she heard him enter the room and put on his blazer, she said, "You can see the Botanical Gardens from here. That's where we're going tomorrow."

Pelham joined her at the window, and she pointed out the gardens. "I'm looking forward to that," he said.

Natalie looked at the clock on the wall. "The cruise ship leaves in forty-five minutes. We should get going. Since parking's a pain, we might want to take a cab. Do you mind?"

"Not at all," Pelham said, grabbing his coat.

Natalie picked up her bag, containing the clothes she had worn that day. "Do you mind if I leave this here and pick it up later? The taxi queue is nowhere near the parking garage, and I don't want to carry it onto the boat."

Pelham hesitated, but then he said, "Sure. You can get it later tonight or wait until tomorrow. Your choice."

Natalie put the bag on the table next to her and headed for the door. Pelham followed her, turning off the lights as he exited the room. *I should offer to come up and get it for her when we return, but it might seem rude to make her wait in the lobby by herself. I need to figure out the right way to handle this.*

They arrived at the dock and were soon onboard the dinner cruise boat. The sunset shining through the windows bathed the dining room in an orange glow as Pelham and Natalie were escorted to their table.

"I love being on the water," Natalie said as they sat. "Seeing the light reflecting off the surface... it's beautiful."

"I agree," Pelham said. "The inner harbor in Baltimore has water taxis to go from one side to the other, and even though I enjoy the walk, I'd rather be on the water, seeing the lights of the city reflecting all around me."

As they waited for the other passengers to board and for the boat to leave the dock, Pelham asked, "So what do you do for fun? And how do you stay so fit, if you don't mind me asking."

"I do yoga for the stretching and for flexibility," Natalie replied, "and I walk, hike, run, and do weights to stay toned. Amir wanted me to stop doing all that so I'd have more time to be with him. But since leaving him, I've gotten back into it, and it feels great. It's not so much that I exercise for my figure; I exercise to feel good. It's fun, and if it ever stops being fun, I'll stop doing it. I don't want to be a slave to some workout routine. What about you? What do you do to stay fit, especially when you travel so much?"

"It's mostly the stress," Pelham joked with a straight face. "Stress keeps me in shape."

Natalie stared at him, not knowing if he were being serious, but when she saw a twinkle in his eye, she laughed. "Actually? You're kidding, right?"

Pelham smiled. "Yes. I run and swim, two things that are easy to do at home and when living out of hotels."

"You've been swimming here?" Natalie asked.

Pelham nodded. "Every morning before breakfast. It's a great way to start the day."

"Do you have a pool at home?"

"Yes," Pelham acknowledged. "I live in the house my parents built before they… before the accident, and they had put in a lap pool. It's outdoors, so I don't use it in the winter months, but they also built a workout room with treadmills and bikes, so I use those in the winter, and then I run the neighborhood and swim in my pool when it's warm outside."

"I've heard that houses in America are huge," Natalie commented.

"Some are, and some aren't," Pelham said. "It all depends on where you live. My last place was a two-bedroom condo that was cramped, but I loved the location. And when I lived in New

Love Lost, Love Found

York City, I paid a fortune for a place smaller than my hotel room here, and that place also had a kitchen and three storage closets in the same space. My parents were smart. They bought the land years ago when the Bethesda area first started growing, and then they didn't develop the property until they were just about ready to retire. They saved a fortune doing it that way, and... well, now it's where I live. Five bedrooms, nine bathrooms, a full office, a gym, a detached guesthouse, six enclosed garages, and 8,550 square feet of living space on three-quarters of an acre. I could never afford a house like that if I had to buy it today. And yet that same house, with the same amount of land, would cost less than a fourth of what it's worth in Maryland if it were in Tennessee, Texas, or Oklahoma. It's all about the location. The farther you're willing to drive to get into the city, the more home you can get for the money."

Natalie nodded. "I've got a lot to learn about living over there, don't I?"

Pelham nodded. "You'll get used to it quickly. Maryland is an expensive market, being so close to DC, but there are reasonable places to live. Like I said, it all depends on how willing you are to drive to get a good price on a home. And rental properties are available almost everywhere. Just remember that the trendier the location, or the closer you live to the entertainment districts, which the younger crowd gravitates toward, the more you're going to pay. Singles pay more to live near the dating scenes. Married couples or families live farther out so they can get more space for the same money."

"Will I make enough as an intern to live somewhere nice?"

Pelham looked confused. "Hasn't anyone discussed salary with you yet?"

Natalie shook her head. "I think they were supposed to before the offer was rescinded. Since it hasn't been officially reinstated, that conversation hasn't happened yet."

Pelham shook his head. "That's not right." He took out a

William Speir

small notebook and pen from his blazer pocket. Then he proceeded to outline the compensation package offered to each intern, which included a corporate apartment at a substantially reduced rental rate. He also outlined what the starting salary would be for the handful of interns offered permanent positions with the firm.

"And that's in U.S. dollars, which is about thirty-five percent more than Australian dollars, based on the current exchange rate," he said when he was finished. "Now let's take a look at what the cost of living is like in Maryland."

He started by showing her what the income taxes were like in Maryland.

"That's all you pay in taxes?" Natalie asked, incredulous. "We pay way more than that."

Pelham grinned. "Welcome to America." He then proceeded to show her the average rents and mortgage payments in the region, along with insurance costs, utility expenses, and other expenses she was likely to have.

Pelham pointed to a number at the bottom of the page. "This is the amount left over each month after taxes and expenses. This is what will cover your personal life, shopping, travel, and so on. Interns get a special rent rate on their corporate apartments, which will hold down your first year's costs considerably, but that'll change if you become a permanent employee. Remember, the lower your rent, the more you'll have left over each month. The same goes for your car payment. The less you finance, the more cash stays in your bank account for other things."

"That's incredible," Natalie said in awe. "I'd have to make over double that here to have anything left over at the end of the month. That's why I used to live in my brother's house, and why I now live in my Aunt's house. I could never afford to live on my own on my salary."

"If you were to live in Baltimore proper, or in the DC area, you'd have to live with two to three roommates to still have this much money at the end of the month," Pelham said, tapping his pen on the number at the bottom of the page. "As I said, it's all about location. The less you pay, the more you keep."

"And what does Maryland look like?" Natalie asked.

Pelham pulled out his phone and showed her photos of the area around his house and the office. "It didn't used to be so developed," Pelham said as he scrolled through the photos, "but there's still a lot of natural beauty all around. I can drive thirty minutes and be in the middle of woods and forests. I can drive the same distance and be across the Potomac River in Virginia and DC, and I'm less than an hour from the Chesapeake Bay."

"Why don't you live closer to the coast?" Natalie asked. "I'd kill to be near the water."

"And you'd pay a fortune for the privilege," Pelham said. "Location, remember? That's the most expensive real estate there is. But for me, the issue is storms. I don't like hurricanes, so I live inland, where the damage from storms is much less."

"Hurricanes? Oh, you mean tropical cyclones," Natalie said. "We have those in Queensland, too. Most of us call them 'willy-willies,' but some places call them typhoons."

"What about snow?"

"In the mountains, sure, but not much around here," Natalie replied.

"We have snow in Maryland," Pelham said. "Lots and lots of snow each winter. You'll have to learn to drive in it, walk in it, dress for it, and clear it off your driveway and sidewalks."

Natalie's eyes went wide. "I've seen it in movies before, but I didn't think it really looked like that south of Canada."

Pelham chuckled. "It does. Oh, the deep south rarely gets much snow, but the Mid-Atlantic, the Northeast, the Upper Midwest get a lot. Of course, it's spring in Maryland right now, and we're moving into the summer months, so you won't have to worry about that until November."

Natalie sighed. "I'm going to have to get used to all the seasons being backwards, aren't I? Christmas is summer down here."

"It's the dead of winter up there," Pelham said. "But that makes it even more beautiful, and a lot of the songs will start making sense once you have your first white Christmas."

Natalie shivered involuntarily. "So much change to get used to. It's a little overwhelming."

"You're not having second thoughts about the internship, are you?"

Natalie sat silently for a moment. "No, not actually. It's just the reality finally hitting me." She cocked her head to one side. "Speaking of which, what about my wardrobe. It's appropriate for the climate in this part of Australia and for the job I do, but is it appropriate for America and the job I'll be doing there?"

Pelham leaned back and looked at her intently. "Different countries definitely have different styles of dress—often dictated by the weather, but also by culture. Australia is a warmer climate, so your clothing tends to be lighter and... well... more revealing. That's perfectly okay away from the office, although the revealing nature of the local attire, like the dress you wore on the first day of the workshop, could attract... shall we say... unwanted attention. The clothing I've seen you wear so far, while perfectly appropriate for your age and your... appearance, is more what we'd consider to be geared for young people who haven't entered into a career yet. For the U.S. workplace, we tend to be a bit more... conservative, more ageless. Our business casual is dressier, and there are times when suits are the most appropriate garments for a business setting. I can send you the recommended minimum wardrobe we give to all interns joining us from outside the U.S."

"Thanks. But what do I do if I don't have any of those wardrobe items?"

"We take you shopping as soon as we get to the States so

Love Lost, Love Found

you can buy them. We're not going to let you get lost in all of the changes that you'll be experiencing," Pelham assured her. "We work hard to help make the transition from your home country to the U.S. a pleasant and easy experience. We don't want you to fail or feel overwhelmed."

Natalie looked relieved. "Thank you for that. It's exciting, but it's scary at the same time. I'm glad someone will be helping me settle in properly."

The boat got underway, and soon they were cruising around the Sydney harbor, looking at the lights. As the first course arrived, Pelham looked at Natalie's face, glowing in the reflection of the city. *What a true beauty she is. She's smart, funny, sweet, and she's much more mature than her years, which makes our age difference almost irrelevant. But I'm the guy who has to decide if she gets the internship, and if anyone ever accuses me of being inappropriate with a candidate, my reputation, and my career, is ruined. Damn.*

Natalie enjoyed the dinner and the sights from the boat. But mostly she enjoyed being with Pelham. He was the first man who had taken the time to explain everything to her in a way that didn't demean her or make her feel overwhelmed. In fact, as overwhelming as the topics they discussed should have been, she actually felt calm and relaxed about making the biggest change of her life—moving to the United States.

And the fact that she found him incredibly handsome didn't hurt things, even if she knew that it complicated things.

Glancing at him while they ate the second course, she thought, *He's handsome, he's kind, he's brilliant... and he's potentially my boss and ten years older than I am. I don't care about the age difference. He and I seem to be on the same level about how we look at things. It's the boss thing that's the* problem. I've never wanted to date a boss before, but I wouldn't mind dating Pelham. He's so different from anyone I've ever been attracted to, but after Amir, he might be just what I've been waiting for... just what I need. I wonder if he feels the same.

They disembarked after the cruise had ended and walked along the dock back to the taxi queue. The wind had picked up, making the air quite chilly. Pelham noticed Natalie walking with her arms crossed, shivering. He took off his outer coat and put it on her shoulders. She pulled it tight and flashed him a grateful smile.

"Thanks, Pelham. That's sweet of you."

Pelham nodded, not realizing that his arm was still around her shoulder, pulling her closer to keep her warm.

Natalie didn't seem to mind.

They rode back to the hotel in silence. When they arrived, Pelham asked, "You left your bag upstairs. Do you want to get it before you leave or wait until tomorrow?"

"Do you mind if I get it now?"

Pelham shook his head. Natalie walked with him to the elevator, and they rode up to his floor.

When they reached his room, Natalie took off Pelham's coat and handed it back to him. "Thanks for this," she said as she picked up her bag.

"You're welcome," Pelham responded. "I'll walk you to your car."

They rode the elevator back to the lobby, and walked to the parking deck. The wind was blowing hard, and Pelham quickly removed his blazer and put it over Natalie's shoulders.

"You seem to be giving me your coats a lot tonight," Natalie joked.

"I hate seeing someone shivering," Pelham said.

Love Lost, Love Found

"What about you? Aren't you cold?"

Pelham shrugged. "Don't worry about me."

They arrived at Natalie's car. She scanned it for trackers, found none, opened the door, and handed Pelham's blazer back to him.

"Thank you for today," Pelham said pleasantly. "I had a great time."

"Are we still on for tomorrow?" Natalie asked.

"I am if you are. Meet here for brunch at ten?"

"I'll be here."

They stared at each other for a minute, each torn between desire and prudence. Finally, Natalie turned to get into her car. Then she suddenly turned back toward Pelham, gave him a kiss on his cheek, and got into her car before he could react. She started the engine, waved to him, and drove off into the night.

Pelham put on his blazer and headed back to the hotel lobby. He touched the cheek she had kissed with his hand as he walked. *Well, that happened. Can we keep things under control, or are we about to break every rule there is?*

Pelham met Natalie the next morning for brunch before they walked over to the botanical gardens. Neither of them mentioned the kiss.

After spending several hours walking through the gardens, and then taking the ninety-minute harbor sightseeing cruise, they returned to Pelham's hotel to plan Natalie's involvement in the workshop scheduled to start the next morning. Even though Pelham worried that it might not be a good idea, it made more sense for them to work in the living room of his suite. When he pointed this out to Natalie, she agreed.

They spent the rest of the afternoon and evening finding the places where Natalie could add the most value to the workshops, both in terms of presenting the workshop material and conducting discussions around certain topics. Pelham's assessment of her performance the previous week led him to believe that she would be a natural at facilitation, so he selected several topics for her to handle, letting him watch and evaluate her performance.

They ordered room service for dinner, and once they felt comfortable with the assignments for the coming week, Natalie left the hotel and returned home.

They met for breakfast each morning that week, and they had dinner together every night. The workshop went incredibly well, and Pelham credited Natalie's enthusiasm for keeping the participants engaged throughout the week.

On Wednesday morning, Natalie had her appointment at the U.S. Consulate, which ended up taking all morning. When she arrived at the meeting-room just after lunch, she was all smiles as she showed Pelham the paperwork she needed to work and immigrate to the U.S. All she needed now was the job offer, so she could get her visa.

That Saturday, they headed to the nearby Marriott to catch transportation for the excursion to the Blue Mountains, west of the city. They spent the day surrounded by the natural beauty of the area, covered in autumn colors, which was hard for Pelham to grasp, given that it was mid-May.

When they returned to Sydney, Pelham and Natalie were both exhausted. "That was the first time I've ever been there," Natalie admitted when the taxi let them out at Pelham's hotel.

"I'm glad it was the first time for both of us," Pelham said as he walked her to her car.

"Why?"

"Because it let me enjoy your reaction as well as my own," he replied. "I've loved the places that you've been to before. You're a great tour guide. But the look of wonder you get when you see something for the first time is great."

Love Lost, Love Found

Natalie blushed. "What time shall I be here tomorrow? This coming week is going to be different from what I've seen, and I need to understand how these sessions work before we decide where I can help you the most."

Pelham nodded. "How about eleven? That will give both of us time to recover from today, and we'll still have plenty of time to go over all the materials for next week."

"Okay. Meet in the lobby?"

Pelham shook his head. "No, we'll meet in my room. I'll order room service for lunch... and dinner if we need it."

Natalie smiled. "Okay. See you tomorrow."

"Good night," Pelham said. "And thanks again for today."

Natalie drove out of the parking deck as Pelham headed for the hotel lobby. *I can't believe how many times I nearly kissed her today. I can't let that happen. Not yet, anyway.*

Chapter 4

Natalie arrived a few minutes before eleven the next morning. The air had turned warm, and she was wearing a pair of shorts and a ribbed T-shirt that hugged her curves snugly. Pelham found her exposed legs very distracting, but he hid his discomfort well.

The upcoming week, Pelham was scheduled to deliver a number of seminars and mini-workshops at The University of Sydney, or Sydney Uni as Natalie called it. There were different sessions for undergraduate and graduate students, and Pelham and Natalie spent hours reviewing the session materials and deciding how Natalie could best help the sessions.

"You're close to their age, so you can speak to them on their level," Pelham said, "but you're also representing Mason, Campbell, Alvarado, & Jürgen, LLP, so you need to appear more experienced than your years. Think you can pull that off?"

Natalie laughed and put on a pair of glasses. "Does this help?"

"It makes you look five years older," Pelham said, grinning. "But I'm afraid the shorts counteract the glasses."

Natalie pouted. "You mean I can't wear this outfit tomorrow?"

"Not if you want the guys in the sessions to pay attention to the material."

Natalie beamed. "I'll take that as a compliment."

"Good, because that's how I meant it."

The sessions at The University of Sydney went without a hitch, and Natalie handled her parts perfectly. She was poised, articulate, and if Pelham didn't already know her age, he would have been convinced that she was closer to thirty.

Friday afternoon, after the last session had ended, Natalie was all smiles about how the week had gone. But as they prepared to leave the campus, Natalie received a text message that changed her whole demeanor.

"Do you mind if we skip dinner tonight?" she asked. "There's something I need to take care of."

"Is everything okay?" Pelham asked, concerned.

"I don't know. I'll tell you all about it tomorrow. Are you okay getting back to your hotel?"

Pelham nodded. "Do what you need to do. But if you need anything, let me know, okay?"

"I will. Thanks."

Natalie walked away, leaving Pelham confused.

Once Natalie was away from Pelham, she re-read the text from Amir, seething. Then she called his number.

"What the hell are you doing texting me, Amir? And how did you get this number?"

"Who's that bloke you're carrying on with, Natalie?" Amir demanded.

"He's my boss, Amir, like it's any of your business."

"It is my business, Natalie. We're soulmates. Our destiny is to be together. You can't just be running around all over Sydney with another guy."

"We're not running around, Amir. He's my boss, and I'm helping him teach workshops and seminars around the city."

"And what were the two of you teaching at the Blue Mountains, Natalie?"

Natalie blanched. *How did he know we went there last weekend?*

"I don't know what you're talking about, Amir."

"You were seen, Natalie. My sister, Ieisha, saw you two. She took a photo and sent it to me." Amir was shouting by this time.

"He needed a tour guide, so I offered. What's wrong with that? I can do whatever I want. It's not like you and I are together anymore."

Amir ignored her. "I'm driving down to Sydney to get you this weekend. Be packed and ready."

"I. Will. Not! If you come near me, I'll call the police and tell them you're trying to kidnap me. Stay away, Amir. I told you we're over, and I meant it."

"Enough of this, Natalie. You've had your fun, but it's time to come home, to come back to me. Got it?"

"No, Amir. I'll never go back to you. Tell your fans that you finally went too far and made me leave you. Then go find someone else you can manipulate and abuse for the fans' entertainment. I'm done. Goodbye."

She ended the call as Amir started shouting at her again. Then she did a quick scan of her phone to see if there were any tracking apps active. She found one, and she deleted it the way Pelham taught her.

She ran to her car and checked it for trackers. She found one inside the front bumper and one inside the rear bumper. She removed them and placed them on nearby cars. Then she drove to the store where she bought her cell phone so she could get her phone number changed and have anti-tracking software installed. It took several hours. By the time she returned to Aunt Rachel's house, she was still anxious. *I wonder what Amir has waiting for me here.*

Fortunately, there were no surprises waiting for Natalie at Aunt Rachel's house. She sent Pelham a quick text with her new phone number, and then she went to find Aunt Rachel and tell her what was going on.

She found her aunt in the kitchen. "Hi, Auntie."

"Hi, Nat," Aunt Rachel said. She was the only person who ever called Natalie "Nat." "You're home earlier than I expected. Have you eaten?"

Natalie shook her head.

"Well, sit down and I'll make you something." She looked at her niece and added, "Is something wrong, sweetie? You seem upset."

"Amir contacted me today." Natalie told Aunt Rachel about the text, the phone call, and all the things Natalie had to do afterwards to keep Amir from being able to track her. "I finally turned the phone off."

"I'm sorry he's bothering you again, sweetie. I used to like him, but what he's doing to you... it proves that he's dangerous and twisted. He's certainly not the man for you."

Natalie nodded. "No, he's not."

Aunt Rachel stared at her niece for a moment. Then she said, "But you've found someone who is the man for you, haven't you?"

Natalie felt her face get flushed. "What makes you say that?"

"Because you've been smiling non-stop for the last few weeks. You glow, and I can still see it, in spite of what Amir did today. It's that guy you've been working with, isn't it? The guy from America?"

Natalie nodded slowly. "I know he's an American, I know he could end up being my boss, I know he's older, and I know he's here to evaluate me for that internship I want. But I'm crazy about him. He's handsome, but that's not it. He treats me... like... like an equal, not like a kid. He listens to my opinions, he makes me want to try harder, he's kind, he seems to want what's best for me... he's the perfect man. I don't know how he feels about me, but he's all I think about. He's the complete opposite of Amir."

Aunt Rachel leaned against the kitchen counter. "I've never seen you like this before, and I know how much you hate rebound relationships. All I'll say is this... be careful. You're in uncharted territory, so don't do anything rash that could jeopardize the job or your heart. Protect both, and keep your eyes and your mind open. Okay?"

Natalie crossed the room and gave her aunt a hug. "Thanks, Auntie. You always know what to say to me."

As Aunt Rachel scurried around the kitchen fixing Natalie something to eat, Natalie wrestled with her thoughts. *I want to be with Pelham, there's no question about that. But I don't like hooking-up, and I refuse to do the naughty to get or keep a job. I did that to keep Amir interested in me, and it turns out that it was just part of how he manipulated me to get what he wanted. Pelham's the kind of guy I want to be in a real relationship with, not another pretend relationship like I had with Amir and the blokes I dated before him. But how can we be in a relationship if we work together? And if we don't end up working together, how can we have any kind of relationship at all besides a hook-up? God, I hate this. It's too complicated. Maybe I just need to step back for a while until things settle down. I don't even know if I'm getting the job. I'll focus on that first and then see what happens.*

When Pelham got back in his hotel room, he called Wes.

"Hi, Pelham. What's up?"

"I have my final assessment of Natalie Patterson to give you," Pelham replied.

"Shoot."

"We want her in the internship program," Pelham stated. "After watching her last week during the workshop at the hotel, and this week at The University of Sydney, I'm more convinced than ever that she's perfect for our firm. No matter what I threw at her, she hit it out of the park."

"You're certain about this?"

"Absolutely. One hundred percent. No doubts at all."

"And do you want her working out of your office?"

"Yes."

"Have you slept with her?"

"No."

"So, this is an honest assessment?"

"Yes, Wes, this is an honest assessment," Pelham assured him. "And you know me better than that."

"I do. I had to be sure. Will she be helping you next week?"

"Yes, and we should get her on the same flight as me, leaving Sydney next Sunday. I'll take the first few days after I get back to Maryland to get her settled and help her acquire a conservative, American-looking wardrobe that's appropriate for our business environment, and then I'll introduce her to the office and get her ready for my meetings in New York, Orlando, and Chicago."

"Okay. That sounds good. Do you want to tell her that she's got the job, or do you want it to come from here?"

"Better if it's official," Pelham said.

"Okay. I'll get the memo out before morning your time. If anything changes between now and when you fly back—"

"Nothing will change, Wes," Pelham stated.

"Fine. Thanks for the info. Let me know how next week goes, okay?"

"I will. Thanks, Wes."

After Pelham ended the call, he stared out the window for a while. *I didn't technically lie to Wes about giving an honest assessment, but I wasn't entirely truthful either. I stand by my assessment, but I can't get Natalie out of my head. If she weren't a candidate for the internship program, and we met socially, there's no question that I'd want to pursue a relationship with her. She's beautiful, she's smart, she's witty, she has gone out of her way to keep me from being alone while I'm here, and she hasn't asked for anything in return. She's sweet, and I forgot what it's like to be with someone who's sweet.*

Pelham watched as colored lights started flashing in the distance. *Well, I've already recommended her for the job, so no one could say that I pressured her so she'd get the job; and she won't be reporting to me, so no one could say that I'm placing undue pressure on her to keep the job. If anything happens between us while we're still in Australia, it's just two consenting adults sharing something beautiful with each other. The only problem is, I don't do one-night-stands, and I don't start things that I can't finish. Hook-ups are for kids. I'm into relationships that are meaningful and mutually beneficial. I want to be with someone who makes me a better person and who is with me for the same reason. What happens when we get back to the States? I know Wes' rules, but rules and emotions don't always agree. Can I have a relationship with someone in my office and still be professional with that person while at work? That's what I have to figure out, because if the answer is no, then this is something that can't go any farther than it has already gone. I won't do that to me, I won't do that to her, and I won't do that to my office. It's not fair to any of us, and it's not right.*

Pelham continued staring out the window, wrestling with the conflicting emotions that were driving him crazy.

The next morning, Natalie arrived at the hotel to pick up Pelham for their day trip to Hunter Valley. Her usual smile was missing as he approached her in the lobby, and the light seemed gone from her eyes.

"What's wrong?" he asked.

"That text I got last night... it was from Amir. He somehow got my number. He also managed to activate tracking software on my phone again and put two trackers on my car. I put the trackers on other cars, deleted the tracking app, and then went to the phone store to change my number and have anti-tracking software installed."

"Are you okay?"

Natalie looked at him in the eyes. "No. I called him back and told him to leave me alone. He asked about you. His sister saw us at Blue Mountain and sent him a photo from her phone. He said he and I are soulmates and he's coming down to bring me back to Brisbane. I told him that I'd tell the police he's trying to kidnap me if he does that. I hung up on him, and that's when I found out he was tracking me again."

Pelham placed a hand on her arm. "Look, we don't have to do the winery tour if you're not up to it."

Natalie smiled. "No, I want to go. I need to be out of the city for a while, and wine never hurts."

Pelham saw the twinkle return to her eye. "Okay. Let's go. The bus picks up about a mile from here. Do you mind if we leave your car here and take a taxi?"

She nodded, and they walked outside to catch a cab.

The bus trip took them through some beautiful country. The tour was limited to six participants, and they proved to be a lively bunch, joking and laughing the whole way out to the valley, which seemed to lift Natalie's spirits.

They visited three small wineries and one distillery that day. In addition to the wine tasting, they had a gin and vodka tasting, paired with cheese and chocolate. The tour also included a lunch and more wine, which Pelham noted that Natalie was enjoying quite a bit. *In her situation, I'd probably be indulging in the wine, too.*

That afternoon, Pelham was introduced to several Australian ciders, which he found excellent. *If I were staying in Australia for another couple of weeks, I'd buy a few bottles of this for the hotel room.*

It was dark before they returned to the bus terminal in Sydney. They hailed a cab back to the hotel.

"Hungry?" Pelham asked.

Natalie nodded.

"Restaurant or room service?"

"Room service. I don't feel like being in a public setting just yet."

"Room service it is, then."

They took the elevator up to Pelham's suite. As he ordered dinner, Natalie sat on the sofa, staring at her phone.

"Why do you keep looking at your phone," he asked when he finished ordering. "Do you expect him to have your new number already?"

Natalie nodded. "He found it before. He could find it again. That's why I have it turned off. Now I'm afraid to turn it back on again."

"You think he could find the new number so soon?"

Natalie shrugged. "I don't know. I still don't know how he found it before. It's like he's trying to prove that there's nowhere I can hide from him. It's so frustrating."

Pelham sat next to her and put his arm around her shoulder, pulling her close. "Well, he can't get to you here and now, so relax. I won't let anything happen to you."

Natalie put her head on his shoulder. "Thanks, Pelham."

Thirty minutes later, there was a knock on the door. Pelham stood and let the room service waiter roll the cart inside with their dinner. The waiter set everything up, Pelham signed the bill, and then the waiter left.

Natalie didn't say much as they ate.

"I had a really good time today, Natalie," Pelham said when he started on dessert. "I'm glad we went."

"Me, too," Natalie said.

After she finished eating, she stood up. "I think I'll head home. What time tomorrow do you want to meet?"

"Noon?" Pelham suggested.

Natalie nodded. "Do you mind if I use your bathroom before I go?"

Pelham gestured toward the bathroom. "As long as you promise to turn your phone on and text me when you get home, so I know you made it."

Natalie smiled and took her phone with her to the bathroom. A moment later, he heard the pinging sound from her phone signaling that she had missed notifications. Then he heard her say, "What? What?" followed by, "Actually?"

She walked out of the bathroom a minute later, eyes wide and smiling. She held up her phone. "I got the job?"

Pelham grinned and nodded. "I called Wes last night and gave him my final recommendation. I told him that you're perfect for the firm. His Internship Coordinator will be reaching out to you this week, and she's going to book you on the same flight to America that I'll be on a week from tomorrow. Now you'll be able to get your visa from the U.S. Consulate. You'll be working out of the Maryland office, if that's okay with you."

Natalie started trembling slightly. "Actually? The job is mine?"

"The job is yours."

She ran forward to the sofa. She was on her knees next to him when she threw her arms around Pelham's neck. Before either knew what was happening, they were kissing. It was electric, and neither wanted to pull away.

Pelham gave in to the feelings that had been building for the past three weeks. He reached down to her left leg and pulled it across him so she was straddling him. His hands began exploring and eventually slid down to cradle her muscular glutes with both hands. A moan escaped her as he gently squeezed. Then his hands moved up to her chest. Her breathing became deeper as she clearly enjoyed what he was doing. She reached down and placed her hand on the part of Pelham that was already growing considerably.

Pelham looked at her. "Are you sure about this? I'm not into casual sex or one night stands. Another minute, and there's no turning back."

"I don't do one nighters or hooking up, either, but I want this more than anything," Natalie whispered. "I want this to be the start of something."

"Me, too." Pelham surrendered. He pulled her shirt up, exposing her bra. Natalie pulled the shirt over her head and then pulled Pelham's golf shirt off. She removed her bra and began kissing him again as his hands cupped her firm breasts.

She undid his belt and the snap of his pants. She pulled down his zipper and reached in, searching for the object of her desire.

Pelham stopped her. "Don't we need…"

Natalie knew what he was going to say. "No. I've got that covered." She had been on the pill since before she'd met Amir.

Pelham let her continue, and when her hand made contact, Pelham felt it stiffen and swell in her hand. Her touch was exhilarating, and all Pelham could think about was giving her the same sensations.

He reached down and unfastened the top of her skinny jeans. He pulled down the zipper and eased the tops of her jeans down, exposing the thong she was wearing. His hands explored

Love Lost, Love Found

her smooth skin, and then he pulled down her thong. He slid his hand down her front and found that she had shaved the area smooth. His hand kept going until it reached her pleasure center. She was already wet from anticipation.

She stroked him as his fingers explored her wetness. Both increased the forcefulness as the sensations became more intense. Then Natalie stood. She stripped and reached down to remove Pelham's clothes. She stood over him admiring his physique. Pelham looked at her unclothed beauty and found his arousal increasing.

Natalie straddled him again and began rubbing herself against him, stimulating him as she lubricated herself. Then she lifted up and guided him inside.

The moment of connection was explosive for them both as he filled every inch of her as no man had before. She moaned loudly and began rising and lowering herself on him. For several minutes, she continued, increasing the speed slowly as she approached her climax. Then she let out a low, gasping moan and leaned back as her stomach muscles spasmed.

Pelham held on to her, keeping her from breaking the connection as she climaxed uncontrollably.

When it was over, Natalie stood, turned around, and sat on Pelham's lap, guiding him in so he was penetrating her again. She rode him in this position until the second climax hit her.

Pelham rolled her off and onto her knees. He stood, and penetrated her from behind, holding on to her waist and pulling her toward him faster and faster. Natalie climaxed two more times as Pelham thrust deeper and faster until he felt his own climax approaching.

"I'm so close," he whispered.

"Don't stop," she whispered back.

His knees began to shake as he felt the threshold approaching. A moment later, he gasped as he reached his release.

"It's so warm," Natalie squealed with delight. "Oh, don't stop."

Pelham kept thrusting, even though he felt like all strength had left him. As the release finally subsided, he pulled out, turned Natalie over, picked her up, and carried her to the bed. He yanked back the covers and set her down, lying next to her. Then he reached over to the nightstand and turned off the lights, allowing the lights from the city to illuminate the suite.

"Oh. My. God!" Natalie said as she snuggled close to him. "That was a total ripper! I'm buggered."

"I assume that means you enjoyed yourself and you're tired," Pelham said. "Feel up for some more?"

Natalie looked up at him. Then she smiled. "Give me a few minutes to catch my breath and I'll be ready to go again."

Pelham wrapped his arms around her, not caring one bit about any rules he had just broken.

They made love again, only this time they moved more slowly to keep the intensity from ending too soon. It was mind-blowing, and Pelham felt like he had been completely drained. He pulled up the covers and began drifting in and out of sleep.

The sun from the open curtains hit him in the eyes several hours later, but that wasn't what woke him up. It was a different sensation taking place much lower.

He glanced down. Natalie had pulled back the sheets and was lying between his legs. Her head was rhythmically moving up and down as her mouth held him captive. He began moaning, and he could tell that she was smiling, in spite of what she was doing to him. Her hands reached up and took his, and as they held on to each other, she increased speed. He felt the suction from the tightness of the seal her lips made coax him toward his biggest climax yet. He began trembling as it got closer. Natalie and Pelham locked eyes as she continued. Just as he didn't think he could take any more, he released, and he heard her sigh with pleasure at what she had accomplished.

Love Lost, Love Found

The spasms continued for more than a minute before they finally subsided. Natalie raised herself onto her knees and smiled at him.

"Good morning, sleepyhead," she said playfully.

Pelham grabbed her and pulled her up beside him. Then he began kissing her body, moving down toward her breasts. Just as he was about to take her left nipple into his mouth, he said, "Your turn."

Natalie grinned and leaned back on the pillow, allowing Pelham to do as he wished.

He kissed and sucked on her nipples, and then he began moving down, kissing and nuzzling her until he was between her legs. He gently kissed her inner thighs. She tried to direct his attention toward where she wanted him to go, but he resisted, teasing her and building the anticipation. When his tongue darted out and found the spot that was waiting for him, she moaned and spread her legs wider so he had unrestricted access to her pleasure center.

Using both his tongue and fingers, he made Natalie climax repeatedly—legs shaking and muscles spasming. She tried to push his head back, but he wouldn't stop. She tried to pull away, but he held onto her. The sensations became more intense than any she had experienced, and though she feared what she was feeling, she surrendered and let him continue. A moment later, she had the most intense climax of her life, shaking uncontrollably and barely holding on to consciousness.

When Pelham finally stopped and moved up beside her, both were covered in sweat.

"How did you do that?" she whispered, unable to speak any louder.

"It's a secret," he whispered back. "If I tell you, you'll tell someone else, and then everyone will know how it's done."

Still panting, she smiled. "Okay. Keep your secret. Thank you for what you just did to me. I don't know if I can walk right now, but thank you anyway. I'll gladly let someone push me around in a wheelchair to feel that again."

"You're welcome."

Two hours later, they had showered, dressed, and were heading downstairs for brunch. Natalie had to hold onto Pelham's arm to steady her as she walked, but neither seemed to mind.

"I was with Amir for four years," Natalie said as the elevator descended to the lobby, "and if you added up all the times we… I *thought* we were making love, it still wouldn't have been as good as last night. I always wondered what it would be like to be with a real man, instead of a man-boy, and last night you showed me. I'm… I'm in awe."

Pelham blushed. "And the age difference doesn't bother you?"

"It's not about the age, it's about the man," Natalie declared. "You don't treat me like a kid, you treat me like a partner, an equal—with kindness, understanding, and respect. No one has ever treated me like that before."

"Well, you deserve to be treated like that," Pelham stated.

As the elevator descended, Pelham suddenly reached out and pressed the floor above the lobby. The elevator stopped and the doors opened. Pelham led Natalie out of the elevator.

"What are we doing here?" she asked, seeing the meeting-room they had used for the workshops in front of them.

Pelham led her to a nearby bench and helped her sit. Then he sat next to her and took her hands in his. "I want to say something, but I don't want to do it in the restaurant. Is that okay?"

Natalie nodded, wondering if they were wrestling with the same thoughts.

"Look, last night was wonderful," Pelham began. "I

wouldn't trade what we shared for anything. But..."

"There are complications?" Natalie finished his sentence.

Pelham nodded. "You see it, too?"

"I do," Natalie replied. "I've been wrestling with it for days. You're the perfect man for me, but you're now technically my boss. How can we make that work?"

"Actually, I'm not your boss. Your boss is the Internship Coordinator. I'm just the person who will assign your work and monitor your performance. I have input, but no control over your employment or your compensation."

Natalie's eyes widened. "Actually?"

Pelham nodded, and he could see thoughts racing through Natalie's mind.

"But what about if I get a permanent position after the internship ends?" Natalie asked. "You'd be my boss then, right?"

Pelham shook his head. "If we're not in a relationship, and as long as we don't pursue one, then you'll report to me. However, if we're already in a relationship, or we're planning to pursue one, it'll be like the internship. I'll assign your work and monitor your performance, but someone else will be your administrative manager—someone in Wes' office. And if our relationship becomes a distraction at work, then you'll be moved to one of the other offices, and we'll have to find a way to make that work."

Natalie thought about this for a while. Then she said, "So, you're saying that we can have a real relationship, with the understanding that it can't affect our work or the people we work with, but are you saying that you'd like to have a relationship with me? Or not? Or maybe?"

"I think I'd like to pursue one, as long as we can keep it out of the office," Pelham replied after a minute.

A hopeful look flashed across Natalie's face. "I think I'd like the same."

They sat next to each other, holding hands, until Natalie's

stomach rumbled.

Pelham laughed and stood. "First things first. Food. Then more relationship talk."

Natalie stood and took Pelham's arm. "Agreed."

CHAPTER 5

The next week was like a whirlwind. In addition to the mini-workshops and seminars at The International College of Management, Sydney, much of the week was spent getting Natalie ready to move to America, which included getting her visa from the U.S. Consulate.

Natalie's parents and brother drove down to Sydney Monday night for a goodbye dinner. After being warned by Natalie about Amir's tricks, they had their phones checked and their cars scanned for tracking apps and GPS tags. None of their phones had been tampered with, but all of their vehicles had GPS tags on them.

Once all of the tags had been removed, Ed, Natalie's brother, came up with the idea to place the tags on the cars owned by Amir's family members. "Let Amir chase Elias, Dasia, and Ieisha for a change," Ed said when they were all at dinner together.

Charles, Natalie's father, spent most of the evening talking to Pelham to understand more about what his daughter would be doing in America. Natalie's mother, Brenda, listened closely, but said very little.

Pelham provided all of the information that the parents

requested, but about any potential personal relationship, he said nothing. *It's not my place to say anything about that.*

Rachel, Brenda's sister, also questioned Pelham about Maryland, about his background, and about him personally, since she knew Natalie was interested in him. Again, Pelham answered all of her questions without revealing what had happened the weekend before. However, Rachel knew that Natalie had not come home Saturday night, and her looks across the table told Pelham that she already had a good idea what was going on.

"What are you going to do wit' your car?" Charles asked with his lilting Irish brogue, after dessert orders had been taken.

"I'm going to sell it," Natalie said. "I can use the cash to get settled in the States, and if I come back, I'll pick up a new one. I don't want any reminders of Amir waiting for me here. And if I stay in America, there's no reason to own a car here that's not being used."

"So, you think you'll stay in America?" Brenda asked, quickly wiping a tear from the corner of her eye.

Natalie nodded. "If I'm offered a permanent position after the internship, I'll take it and stay there. If I don't get offered a permanent position," she added, glancing at Pelham, "I'll stay to see if there's anything for me in the area before deciding whether or not to come back here."

"You're taking my baby girl away from us," Charles growled at Pelham.

"No, he's not, Dad," Natalie said. "I wanted this job long before Pelham came here."

Charles looked at his daughter. "Well, don't expect me to be pleased about t'is. It's bad enough you left Brisbane, but now you're leaving t'is hemisphere!"

"Just like you did when you moved here from Galway, Ireland, Dad," Natalie pointed out.

"T'at's different," Charles muttered.

"Too right, because it's what you wanted," Natalie accused him. "This is what I want, and while you may not like it, I know it's what's best for me."

"You'll forget about us," Charles said, sounding glum.

Natalie snorted. "Like that could ever happen. Besides, we'll have weekly video chats like we've been doing since I moved to Sydney. That won't change."

Charles nodded slowly. Looking at Natalie, he asked, "So, t'ere's no changing your mind about t'is?"

"None," Natalie said, shaking her head.

Dessert arrived, and the conversation shifted to happier topics.

Once dinner was over, and everyone had hugged Natalie several times, Natalie's parents and brother left for their hotel and Aunt Rachel returned home. Natalie drove Pelham back to his hotel.

"Sorry about my parents," she said as they drove through the city. "They're a little… overprotective—especially after the whole Amir business."

"It's not a problem," Pelham said. "It's to be expected, when your youngest child is about to move across the globe."

Natalie accelerated through an intersection. "We have so much to get done this week."

"I know, and I want to talk to you about that."

"Okay."

"Tomorrow's seminars end at noon. Why don't we take care of selling your car tomorrow? There must be dealerships that buy used cars around here, right?"

"Yes," Natalie confirmed. "But if we sell my car, how will we get around town?"

"I'll arrange for a car service to take us and pick us up. That's what I was planning to do, until you offered to drive me around, so it's already in the budget for this trip."

"And will you come and pick me up and drop me off at

Aunt Rachel's all week?"

"I was thinking about getting you a room at my hotel, so we're both there. That way, the car service only has to pick us up and drop us off at a single location, and you'll have all your stuff there that you're taking on the plane Sunday."

"Why don't I just stay with you?" Natalie asked.

"I didn't want to presume that's what you wanted," Pelham said. "But if it is, we can make that work."

"It would save the company the cost of the room for five nights," Natalie pointed out.

"Good point. Look at you, already trying to save the company some money!"

Natalie laughed. "Yes, that's why I made that suggestion."

Pelham chuckled. "Okay. So, once your car is sold, we'll need to figure out what you're taking to America. Do you have enough luggage for all your things?"

"No," Natalie admitted. "When I moved down here in March, most of my things were in boxes."

"How many boxes?" Pelham asked.

"Twelve, I think."

"And how many will you need for America?"

"Maybe ten."

Pelham thought about this. "Okay. We'll get new boxes and pack them very carefully, so everything fits in them and the luggage you have that you're taking on the plane. Then we'll check the boxes with your luggage, pay the extra fee, and that way you'll have all your things with you when we get to Maryland. It'll be better to do that than to ship your things, and much less expensive."

Natalie thought about it for a bit. "Or, since I'm going to be buying new clothes once I get over there, why don't I only take my favorite things with me. You know, what I like to lie around the house in, what I exercise in, some of my nicer clothes, things like that. I could probably get everything packed in suitcases, if I bought one or two more large ones. I could have Aunt Rachel donate the rest."

"That's entirely up to you," Pelham said. "I would also advise not packing anything electronic. We're on different power over there, and adapters don't really work that well. We can replace those items when we get your new clothes."

"Well, that'll free up space in my luggage," Natalie said. "What about my laptop?"

"Bring it, and if we can't have the power cable adapted for U.S. power, we'll get you a new one, like we will with your phone. The place I shop for computers should be able to transfer all of your files over to the new machine, and they'll be able to make certain that Amir doesn't have any surprises hidden on your current laptop."

Natalie drove in silence for a few minutes. Then she said, "Tomorrow's going to be a busy day."

The Tuesday seminar at The International College of Management, Sydney, went well. Natalie and Pelham grabbed a quick lunch on campus and then headed for the store where Natalie was buying the extra luggage she needed. Then they headed for the car dealership she wanted to use to sell her car.

"You know they're going to treat me like a girl instead of a serious customer," Natalie commented as they approached the dealership.

"Do you want some help?" Pelham asked.

"Yes, please. You'll probably get a better deal than they'd give me."

"No worries. Leave everything to me," Pelham said reassuringly. "Just play along with whatever I say or do."

Curious, Natalie pulled into the dealership and found a place to park. Then she followed him inside.

"I want to see someone about selling a car," Pelham stated to the receptionist.

"Of course, sir," the receptionist said.

A minute later, a man barely older than Pelham walked up. "I understand you want to sell a car."

Pelham gestured toward Natalie. "She does. I'm here to make certain that she's given a fair price. If I think she's not being treated with the proper respect, I'll end this. The same goes for a deal that's not in her best interest. Okay?"

The car dealer seemed taken back by what Pelham said, but he recovered quickly. "Of course, sir. Let's take a look at the car, shall we?"

Natalie led the man to the parking lot.

Over the next forty-five minutes, the car dealer and his chief mechanic examined the car and test-drove it to make certain there were no issues with the components.

When they met in the dealer's office, he said, "Well, the car is in amazing shape and should sell quite easily. It's a popular model and highly desirable year. I think we can make you a very generous offer." He wrote a number on a piece of paper and slid it across the table to Natalie.

Pelham looked at the number and snorted. "Too low," he said. He had already researched what the car would be sold for, and while he knew that everyone needed to make a profit, the dealer didn't need to make that much profit.

The dealer protested, but Pelham glared at him sternly. "Too. Low. Try again."

The dealer's eyes darted back and forth from Natalie to Pelham. He wrote another number down and slid that across the table.

Pelham looked at it. "Better, but what about this?" He took the piece of paper, scratched through the number and wrote a different number in its place.

When he slid the new number back to the dealer, the man

looked at it and blanched. He looked at Pelham and Natalie, who were both staring at him with blank expressions on their faces.

The man winced and then said, "Fine. Do you want the money applied to another purchase?"

"She wants cash," Pelham said, "But she'll take a cashier's check that has no holds on it so it can be cashed immediately."

"Immediately?"

"As in today," Pelham said flatly.

"And you have all of the paperwork on the car?" the dealer asked.

Natalie slid a folder across the table containing the title and proof that Natalie was the owner and that there were no outstanding loans or liens on the vehicle.

The dealer nodded and picked up the phone to call the accounting department. After a few minutes, a young woman arrived and presented a check to the dealer. He reviewed it, nodded to the woman, and handed the check to Natalie.

"I believe this covers the price we agreed upon."

Pelham examined the check to make certain that no additional fees were deducted from the total. Seeing none, he nodded to Natalie.

Natalie placed the check in her purse and handed the car keys to the dealer. "Thank you very much. It was a pleasure doing business with you."

"The pleasure was all mine," the man said, shaking her hand. He turned to shake Pelham's hand, but Pelham had already left the office and was walking toward the receptionist's desk.

When he reached the receptionist, he said to her, "Would you mind calling for a taxi please?"

The woman nodded and called a local service.

Natalie removed all of her personal items from her old car, along with the luggage she had purchased earlier. Twenty minutes later, they were in the taxi, heading for Natalie's bank, so she could deposit the check. Then the taxi took them to Aunt

Rachel's house.

They spent the rest of the afternoon packing Natalie's things. By the time they were done, everything that Natalie was taking to the United States fit into one large and two medium roller bags, one garment bag, and one carry-on bag that contained her laptop.

Pelham called the hotel, which dispatched their limo to Aunt Rachel's house to pick them up. As they waited for the limo to arrive, Pelham helped Natalie box up the items she was leaving behind—which included the rest of the clothes that Amir had bought her over the years—and move the boxes into Aunt Rachel's garage.

When the limo arrived, Pelham took Natalie's suitcases and bags to the car, while Natalie said goodbye to her Aunt.

"He seems like a good man," Rachel whispered to Natalie as they hugged. "You two seem good together. I hope it works out. You deserve to be happy."

"I am happy, Auntie. But I'll keep you posted."

"You'd better."

Natalie saw Pelham waiting for her. She gave Rachel a quick kiss and then ran to the car. A moment later, the limo pulled away from the curb and headed back to the Hilton.

That night, Pelham helped Natalie open an account at his bank using their online system. The money that Pelham had paid her for her time working with him, the money she had saved to pay for her master's degree program—which she ended up not using—the money from the sale of her car, and her other savings were all in one account at her bank in Sydney. The next morning, she'd wire those funds to the bank in Maryland.

"It's a pity that the Australian dollar is only worth sixty-three cents in America," she lamented and they sat next to each other on the couch in their suite.

"At least what my firm paid you for your time was in U.S. dollars," Pelham reminded her.

"That's true."

"Besides, you made a sizeable profit selling your car, so even with the exchange rate, you'll be starting out with a good amount in your account."

"That I'll be spending on new clothes and the other items I have to replace."

Pelham smiled. "Moving isn't easy, but I think you're doing everything the best way possible, and you're handling it all quite well."

"That's because you're here to help," Natalie said. "If I was doing this myself, I'd be a total wreck."

"Glad I was here, then."

The remaining workshops and seminars all went well. Pelham had Natalie conduct at least half of the sessions, and she did a great job.

Pelham felt strange sharing his suite with Natalie, but he also enjoyed having her there. It had been a very long time since he had just slept with someone and had someone sharing his space. It took a bit of getting used to, but by the end of the week, it seemed perfectly natural. He loved waking up next to someone, but he was worried about what would happen once they left Australia. *I wonder how we should handle living arrangements when we get to Maryland.*

On Saturday, they hung out at the hotel, resting from the grueling schedule that week and preparing for the trip home.

On Sunday afternoon, the hotel limo drove them to the Sydney Kingsford Smith International Airport for the twenty-one-hour trip to Washington-Dulles. Natalie was a bundle of nervous excitement as they waited to board their flight. To avoid embarrassing her, Pelham fought the urge to laugh. *She's making the biggest change of her life, and this is how she's processing what's happening to her. I don't want to make her feel bad or self-conscious. She's embarking on a great adventure. My job is to be supportive.*

What Pelham had not told her yet, though, is that Amir had decided to take drastic action to keep tabs on what Natalie was up to. Pelham had been monitoring Amir's social media accounts to see if he would share his frustration that he could no longer track Natalie's phone, car, or possessions. He did.

Amir posted a video to each of his social media accounts.

"Hello, everyone. This is Amir. As you may have noticed, I haven't been posting any videos on my main channel lately. That's because Natalie moved to Sydney and has been ghosting me. No, it's not because of anything that I did. She's been hanging out with some people who are clearly leading her astray. I wouldn't say that they're part of a cult or anything like that, but they've driven a wedge between her and everyone who loves her—her family, her friends, and me. I need to get her away from these people, but I don't know where she is. I need your help. Here is the most recent photo I have of her." Amir showed Natalie and Pelham on their excursion to the Blue Mountains. "My sister took this picture. I have no idea who the guy is that she's with in the picture, but he might be involved with her disappearance. If any of you see either of these two people, please send me a private message through any of my social media accounts. It could just save her life. Thanks."

Pelham knew that Amir had over 2.5 million social media followers around the world, potentially placing Natalie at risk of discovery anywhere she went. Pelham had already downloaded a copy of the video to share with Natalie once they were away from Australia, and he dreaded having to show it to her.

Who needs GPS trackers when you can tap into millions of

fans? Pelham glanced around the departure lounge. *There could be people here who have recognized us and told Amir where we are. There could be people who'll recognize us when we change planes in Dallas-Fort Worth or once we arrive at Washington-Dulles. She could be spotted buying clothes in Maryland, going to and from the office, or when we're traveling to New York, Orlando, or Chicago. Short of changing her appearance, there's nowhere she can go where she's not at risk of being recognized. And now he has people looking for me, too. Wes will be furious when he finds out, but I have to tell him anyway, meaning that I'll have to give him the full background on Natalie's relationship with Amir. It could influence his decision about keeping her in the internship program or offering her a permanent position when the program is over. What a mess.*

Pelham typed a quick email to Wes and attached the video to it. The email read: "Hi Wes, the attached video was posted to social media by a man named Amir Dimitrios, who is Natalie Patterson's ex-boyfriend. He's dangerously obsessed with her. In fact, he's the reason she missed her original consulate appointment. He has been tracking her using GPS tags and apps on her phone. I helped Natalie locate them and disperse them all around Sydney to keep him from knowing where she is. Now he's using social media to find her—2.5 million fans/subscribers world-wide. The photo he posted is one of Natalie and me from one of the weekends where she was showing me around Sydney, meaning that my face is also visible in the video. This is not Natalie's fault, so I hope you don't hold it against her. It's not my fault either, but I have inadvertently put the firm in a precarious position, and for that I'm sorry. Watch the video and let me know what you think we should do. Natalie works for us now, so we need to do what's right for her and for the firm. We're at the airport now, and we'll be in Maryland late tonight. I'm taking Natalie shopping for new clothes tomorrow (nothing she has is appropriate for the job), but I'll be available by phone all day. I'll also try to call you during our layover in Dallas-Fort Worth. Talk soon, Pelham."

Pelham turned off his phone and put it in his briefcase. *This whack-job Amir is obsessed, and that makes him dangerous. I'll need to beef up the security around my home, the office, and wherever Natalie ends up living.*

The voice over the public address system said: "Qantas Airlines flight to Dallas-Fort Worth, Texas, is ready for boarding. First class and business class passengers may board at this time."

Pelham was so deep in thought that he missed the boarding announcement for their flight.

Natalie shook his arm. "Didn't you hear? They just called our flight."

Pelham smiled. "Sorry about that. I just had to send a quick update to Wes." He stood and grabbed his carry-on bag. "Are you ready?"

Natalie sprung to her feed and grabbed her carry-on. "I think so." The smile on her face was infectious.

"Then let's go."

He led her to the jetway, where he and Natalie presented their boarding passes to the attendant. They were allowed to proceed onboard and quickly located their business class seats.

Once seated, Pelham looked at Natalie. She appeared nervous, but she was grinning. "Don't like flying or nervous about leaving Australia?" he asked.

"Leaving Australia," Natalie said.

"Having second thoughts?"

Natalie shook her head. "No, just remembering that the last time I flew was returning from Seoul after Amir made me miss my Consulate interview. Not the happiest memory."

"You're making new memories now," Pelham reminded her.

Natalie's face lit up, and she nodded.

Love Lost, Love Found

Pelham patted her hand and leaned back in his seat. *It's a good thing she doesn't know what Amir's up to just yet. I want to talk to Wes before I let her know, but it's likely that she'll find out from one of her friends or relatives before then. I'll tell her when we're waiting to change planes in Dallas-Fort Worth. No sense adding to her angst right now.*

At three-forty in the afternoon, Sydney time, the cabin doors closed and the airplane pulled away from the terminal.

"Here we go," Natalie said. She turned to Pelham. "Thank you… for everything."

Pelham smiled, but inside, he worried about what Wes would do once he saw the video.

Chapter 6

The fifteen-and-a-half hour flight to Texas was smooth, but long. Pelham and Natalie napped between the food and beverage services, but they also chatted quietly about the living arrangements once they reached Maryland.

"The email I received from someone named Beverly Houston—"

"That's the Internship Coordinator," Pelham interjected.

"Oh. I wondered who she was." Natalie continued. "The email said that the firm has arranged a corporate apartment near the office for the duration of the internship, and I'll be expected to pay half of the rent, while the firm pays the other half."

"That's the standard deal we make with all interns, since they get a reduced salary in lieu of the training they receive," Pelham reminded her.

Natalie nodded. "She also suggests that I lease a car, which will be cheaper than purchasing one, especially if I don't get offered a permanent position at the end of the program."

"We have corporate discounts at a couple of dealerships, which should help hold down the costs."

Natalie smiled. "Your firm really does know how to make things easy on us, doesn't it?"

Love Lost, Love Found

Pelham grinned. "What's the point of attracting top talent from around the world, if we don't treat them right once they arrive? If you want the best, you need to treat them like the best."

"So, you think I'm one of the best?" Natalie asked coyly.

"You wouldn't be sitting next to me right now if I didn't."

"And what we've been doing at night—"

"Has absolutely nothing to do with my decision," Pelham said flatly.

"Will we be able to continue that once we get to Maryland?" Natalie asked softly.

Pelham looked at her. "We'll have to be careful. No one can know that we're involved, so whatever we do, it can't be obvious to anyone. That means that, at the office, I'll have to treat you just like I treat the rest of my staff. Now, the good news is that I treat my staff very well, but I can't make it look like I'm playing favorites. A lot of our office interactions will have to be an act to keep up appearances. Can you handle that?"

"I hope so," Natalie said.

"And if I say or do something that hurts you," Pelham added, "we can talk about it away from the office. Just know that I'll never do that on purpose, okay?"

Natalie nodded. "Are all office romances this complicated?"

Pelham shrugged. "I have no idea. I've worked very hard to never have one, so I'm in uncharted territory, too. We'll just have to find ways that work for us, and hopefully the joys of being together will outweigh the complexities."

Natalie snuggled up next to him and held onto his arm.

"Oh, and I should warn you about something."

"What?" she asked.

"Most of my staff are guys. Between your accent, which is delightful, and your looks, I'd be surprised if some of them didn't start hitting on you."

"Hitting on me?"

"Trying to date you," Pelham explained.

Natalie giggled. "You think I'm that good looking?"

"To the point of distraction," Pelham responded. "And your accent is hypnotic. No American guy will be able to resist you."

Natalie shook her head. "But I'm so ordinary. In Australia, I'm considered average."

"Not where we're going. In America, you're going to turn heads wherever you go."

"That's just weird."

Their plane touched down at Dallas-Fort Worth Airport shortly after four in the afternoon, local time.

"It's only twenty-five minutes after we left Sydney," Natalie noted as she adjusted her watch for local time, "but we were in the air for over fifteen hours. That's bizarre."

They grabbed their carry-on bags and exited the plane. Their next stop was baggage claim, where they had to retrieve all their bags before heading to immigration.

An hour later, they had passed through immigration with no issues, rechecked their bags for the flight to Washington-Dulles, and were sitting in the departure lounge for their next flight. Natalie found the experience interesting. She had flown international flights before, but never as anything other than a tourist. Entering the country as a potential immigrant was a different procedure, but everything went smoothly.

Once they were seated near the departure gate, Pelham stepped away to call Wes.

"It's me," he said when Wes answered the phone.

"That was a hell of a video," Wes said. "It was the act of a desperate person with enough smarts and internet savvy to be dangerous. No wonder Natalie wants to get far away from him."

"What do you want to do?"

Love Lost, Love Found

"Has she seen the video yet?"

Pelham looked over at Natalie, who was looking at the people walking past. "I don't think so. Not yet."

"She should see it as soon as possible," Wes stated. "Once she has, call me so the three of us can put our heads together."

"You're going to support her?" Pelham was surprised, but happy.

"Absolutely. She's part of the team now, and we take care of our own. Plus, we're an advertising firm that also does publicity work. If we can't help her spin this in her favor, we have no right to be in this business, do we?"

"Point well taken."

"Is there anything else you need to talk to me about before she sees the video?" Wes asked.

"Ummm... yes?"

"You didn't."

"I did," Pelham confessed. "It wasn't planned... well, the first time wasn't planned."

Wes laughed. "Oh, buddy, it happens to the best of us. Do you still want her working with you?"

"Yes. We've talked, and we'll find a way to keep it out of the office."

"That's all I ask. We'll talk more when it's convenient. Show her the video, and then call me back."

"Thanks, Wes."

Pelham ended the call and walked back to Natalie.

"Everything okay?" she asked when he sat next to her.

"Not exactly," Pelham said. "There's something I need to talk to you about. There's a problem that I discovered right before we left Sydney. It's not a problem with you, but it affects you. It's a problem with Amir, or at least, it looks like he's trying to cause a problem."

"What? What?" Natalie now looked angry and scared.

Pelham queued up the video on his phone. "Watch this, and

then we'll talk."

Pelham pressed play, and Natalie watched as Amir attempted to mobilize his fans to track her down.

When the video was over, Natalie looked at Pelham with a distressed expression on her face. "Oh, my God. What am I going to do?"

There were tears building in Natalie's eyes, and Pelham handed her a handkerchief.

As she was struggling to regain her composure, Pelham said, "Look at me, Natalie." She did. "You're not going through this alone. This is what I was talking to Wes about a few minutes ago. I sent him a copy of the video—"

"Your boss knows? God, Pelham, he must be ready to put me back on a plane to Australia right now."

"No, he's not. You're a member of the team, and we take care of our own. He fully supports you, as do I. He wants us to call him, so we can figure out the best way to handle this. As he reminded me when I called him, we're a top advertising firm that also does publicity work. If we had a client dealing with a situation like this, we'd craft a campaign to turn the narrative around so that the client comes out on top. Wes and I are going to do the same with you, and you're going to help us."

Natalie dried her eyes and stared at Pelham. "You and your boss are going to help me? How?"

"That's what we're going to figure out." In that moment, Pelham had an idea. "Look at it this way. Amir is tapping into his social media followers. Now, apart from the subscribers to his video channel, you have almost the same number of social media followers as he does, and I'd be willing to bet that many of them are the same people."

Natalie nodded.

"So, if we tap into your social media followers to present your side of the story, how long do you think it would take to reach most if not all of the people who saw his video?"

Natalie frowned as she thought about what Pelham was suggesting. "A day. Maybe two. But he has accounts on some platforms that I don't."

"How long would it take to create an account on those platforms?"

"A few minutes," Natalie said.

Pelham smiled. "Then get started, and I'll call Wes."

Natalie smiled for the first time and pulled out her phone. She turned it on, ignoring the notifications that came flooding in from her existing social media accounts.

Pelham dialed Wes' number.

"She's seen the video," Pelham said when Wes answered.

"How did she take it?" he asked.

"Like you'd expect, but I had an idea, and she's working on it now." Pelham outlined what he was thinking.

"That's what I'd expect from a partner," Wes said proudly. "Turn the situation around, using the same methods and tools."

Natalie looked up. "Done," she said. "What next?"

Pelham turned on the speaker so Natalie could hear Wes. "Are you up for creating a video to post to all of your accounts?" Pelham asked.

"Actually?"

"I think it's a great idea, Natalie," Wes said. "Post a rebuttal video that tells your side of the story. Hold nothing back. Humiliate that demented prick and show him that he's messing with the wrong person when he comes after you. Let your army of followers defend you against his army of followers, and tag him on your posts so it shows up in his feed, too. He'll see it, his followers will see it, your followers will see it, and he'll have some serious explaining to do."

Natalie smiled, but then she got a worried expression on her face. "He won't take it well. He'll escalate this, once he figures out how."

"Possibly," Wes said. "But he's just one person, and you've

now got the entire firm helping you. After all, if we can't help one of our own, how can we help our clients? This is what we do, and you're now our client, too."

"I can't thank you enough for that, Wes. You hardly know me. I wouldn't blame you if you sent me off just to avoid the whole mess."

"That's not what we do, Natalie," Wes assured her. "And even though what I know about you came from Pelham's recommendations, I know him, and I trust him. If he's behind you, then so am I, and so is the entire firm."

"Thank you," Natalie said again.

"Okay," Wes said. "Do this. Make the video there in the airport and send it to me. I'll watch it and provide critiques, if necessary. Then post it to all of your accounts, cross referencing all of your other accounts, and make certain that Amir, all mutual friends, his family, and your family are tagged. Then sit back and see what happens. If we need to take additional action, we will, but let's start with this."

"Okay," Natalie said.

"We'll call you back when the video is ready," Pelham added. "Talk soon."

Pelham looked at Natalie. She no longer seemed distressed, she seemed resolute. "Do you know what you're going to say?"

She nodded. "Will you hold the camera for me?"

"Of course."

"Then let's do this."

Pelham took her phone, took a seat across from her, and hit the record button. Then he nodded to her.

"Hello everyone, this is Natalie. By now, you all should have seen that piece of rubbish video that my ex-boyfriend, Amir, posted to his social media accounts. Actually, I shouldn't call it rubbish because that's an insult to videos that actually are rubbish. Perhaps I should have called it a crap-load of half-truths and out-and-out lies. Here's the truth.

Love Lost, Love Found

"First of all, when Amir says that he didn't do anything to make me leave him, that was a whopper of a lie. For four years, he has manipulated me and emotionally abused me. The final straw broke when I had a job interview for an internship in America the same week as the video content creator's conference in Seoul, Korea. He hacked my phone and changed my calendar, so I'd miss that interview and fly to Korea with him. I was so angry when I realized what he had done, that I left him as soon as I received notification that the interview had been missed and the job offer had been rescinded. By the time he returned to Brisbane, I already knew that it was over between him and me. I decided to move to Sydney to get away from him. I told him to his face that it was over and that I was leaving him, and he started going on and on about us being soulmates and that he'd never let me go. But we're not soulmates; he just doesn't want to lose his control over me. If my brother hadn't been there to protect me, Amir would never have let me leave.

"I worked very hard to re-earn the position in America, which required in-person assessments and interviews to make certain that I was still a good risk and not some flighty girl who was unreliable. I explained why I missed the original interview, and the company understood that it was not my fault. In the end, the job offer was restored.

"Now let me tell you the real reason Amir is using all of you to do his dirty work. He installed tracking software on my phone—not just one app, but multiple apps. He also put GPS tags in my purse, in and on my car, and in all the luggage I ever used when he and I were together. I found over a dozen GPS tags that he was using to cyberstalk me. Well, I had a little fun at his expense. I put those tags on delivery trucks, garbage trucks, police cars, and other vehicles that would make it impossible for him to know where I was. My family also found tags on their vehicles, and they put them on the vehicles owned by Amir's family. Amir is an obsessed tosser who humiliated me, ripped my heart out with his stupid, childish pranks, and has terrorized me since moving to Sydney. He used to stand across the street from where I live, just staring. He showed up at my work. He stood on street corners that I drove past. He waited for me when I left pubs and restaurants. If anyone is a cult, it's Amir, and any of you who are helping him right now are part of that cult. You need to get help and get as far away from him as you can. He's dangerous, he's gone completely troppo, and he's going to escalate until something terrible happens. Don't be a part of it."

Natalie gestured around her. "Right now, I'm in Texas. My flight landed here just over an hour ago. I didn't ghost Amir, I escaped from him, but the experience in Sydney taught me that I'm not safe anywhere in Australia. So, I moved halfway across the world for two reasons: I have a great job, and it's as far from Amir as I can get on this planet. I will never go back to him. I feel nothing but contempt for him. He has been lying to you, just like he lied to me for four years. He never loved me, he only loved what he could do to me to entertain his fans. And now that I'm gone, he wants me back, but that's never going to happen.

"If you see me somewhere, don't bother telling him where I am. It'll do him no good. And if you ever do see me with him again, just know that he had to kidnap me to make it happen, because it will never happen of my own free will.

"Take care, and God bless. This is Natalie signing off from America. Cheers."

Pelham ended the video and sent a copy to his phone. Then he stood and handed Natalie's phone back to her.

"Fantastic! But what did you mean that he's gone troppo?"

"That means he's gone crazy." Natalie stood up and hugged him. "That felt good. Do you think Wes will like it?"

"Let's find out." Pelham forwarded the video to Wes. Five minutes later, Wes called.

"What did you think?" Pelham asked when he answered, turning on the speaker so Natalie could hear the conversation.

"I am impressed!" Wes said. "It was powerful, it was direct, and it was sincere. It should blow up social media in no time."

"Does it need any changes?" Pelham asked.

"No. Post it, and let's see what happens."

Natalie smiled and gave Pelham a thumbs-up. Then she started uploading the video to all of her media accounts, adding a series of hashtags in the headings to help make her point about Amir being a deranged liar.

Pelham stepped away from Natalie and turned the speaker off so no one could overhear. "You think this'll work?"

"For now, but if he's anything like she described, this is just the first round."

"I'm sorry about this, Wes. I know it's not her fault, but I'm sorry you're having to deal with it."

"Don't worry," Wes said. "Shit happens. I imagine you're going to keep a close eye on her and keep her safe."

"That's the plan."

"Do you love her?"

Pelham looked over at Natalie, who was still uploading the video. "Let's say I'm falling in love with her. It's hard not to."

"Well, I trust you, Pelham. Don't let me down."

"I know the risks and the consequences, Wes. I'll keep them firmly in mind."

"Good. Well, enjoy your flight home. I'll stop by the office with Beverly sometime after you and Natalie get back from your next round of workshops and seminars."

"Sounds good. I'll call you later this week before we head to New York."

Pelham ended the call and sat down next to Natalie. She was smiling as she kept uploading the video. When she was done, she started reading through the notifications that were waiting for her when she first turned on her phone.

After a few minutes, she said, "Most of these notifications are from people trying to warn me about what Amir is up to.

Looks like a lot of people have my back."

"What about the rest of the notifications?"

"They're mostly Amir's die-hard fans who are trying to convince me to just go back to him and start making videos with him again. I hope they get used to disappointment."

Pelham laughed.

Natalie read and cleared off all of the notifications, and then she turned off her phone and put it in her carry-on bag.

"Feel better?" Pelham asked.

"You have no idea how much better."

The gate agent announced that their flight to Washington-Dulles would be boarding in five minutes.

"We'll be in Maryland in four hours," Pelham said. "The keys to your corporate apartment are locked in Lauren's desk, so I can't get them until tomorrow, at the earliest."

"Lauren?"

"My Admin and Office Manager. I guess that means you'll have to stay with me until we go by the office."

Natalie beamed. "I've wanted to see your house ever since you told me about it. Are you sure you're okay with that?"

Pelham nodded. "Remember, I have five bedrooms plus a guesthouse. If anyone askes, you stayed in the guesthouse."

"Is that where I'll actually be staying?"

"No, but that's what we'll tell anyone who asks. Okay?"

Natalie laughed. "Got it. Our secret."

Pelham saw the first class and business class passengers queueing up close to the gate. He stood and motioned for Natalie to do the same. They grabbed their carry-ons and headed for the gate just in time to hear the boarding announcement for their flight. In less than five minutes, they were onboard and in their seats, waiting for the rest of the passengers to board, so the plane could depart.

CHAPTER 7

Just before 11:00 PM local time, their flight landed at Washington-Dulles airport. It had been a long day of traveling, and both Natalie and Pelham looked forward to getting home and crawling into bed.

Natalie turned on her phone while they waited for their luggage at baggage claim. Pelham heard the notification chimes, telling her that people were commenting on her video.

Pelham watched Natalie scroll through the notifications, and he saw her smile.

"People love the video we posted. They're ripping Amir in their comments and vowing to unsubscribe from his video channel. They totally believe that he lied in his video, and they believe me."

"How does that make you feel now?" Pelham asked.

"Powerful," Natalie replied, looking surprised at her own answer. "I feel... free."

"Any negative comments?" Pelham asked.

"Not really negative comments, but some of his die-hard fans think his video and mine are all part of an act—a major prank that we're playing on them. People can be so stupid."

Pelham nodded.

"Uh oh, here's a private message from Amir himself."

"What does he say?" Pelham asked.

Natalie read Amir's comment to Pelham. "Jesus, Natalie, what the hell are you doing? You can't say things about me on social media. It'll hurt the video channel. You know how important that channel is. You need to take down your video, right now. What were you thinking? This has gone on long enough, Natalie. Stop acting like a child, stop this nonsense, and call me so we can work through your problems. I swear, if something you've done hurts my channel, I'll make you regret it. Call me. Now."

Pelham laughed. "Is that video channel really so important to him?"

"It's everything to him," Natalie said. "He had it before he and I ever met. He lives for his subscribers, who constantly suggest pranks for him to pull and who he should pull them on. You wouldn't believe some of the things he did to me just because one of his fans put him up to it. It's his identity, his ego booster. It's all he truly loves in life."

"Good to know," Pelham commented. "If he attacks you again, then that's where we need to target our response."

"How do you mean?" Natalie asked.

"Well, what would happen if you made the company hosting his channel take down every video that had you in it?"

"He'd lose his mind. That's the content that's making him money right now. But he told me several times he doesn't need my permission to post videos of me and there's nothing I can do to make him take them down."

"Did you take him at his word or research it yourself?"

Natalie stared at him, wide-eyed. "Ummm, I took him at his word. Why?"

"Because you usually have to secure someone's permission to post their image publically—especially if you're doing it for money. Did he ever pay you from the proceeds of his channel's monetization?"

"No. He bought me gifts and took me to conferences, but he never shared the money he made from the channel with me."

"That might be enough to force him, or the channel's hosting company, to remove all that content. I'll have my lawyers look into it, but I believe there's something we can do, if he won't let you go."

The baggage claim conveyor started turning, and Pelham and Natalie turned to watch for their bags.

"You might also want to consider changing the privacy settings on your social media accounts," Pelham suggested. "If most of your followers are also Amir's followers who are just following you because of the videos, then they can't be trusted. You might want to consider limiting who can see your posts to family and close friends who you actually know. After all, someone gave him your new number in Sydney, and you don't want that to happen again."

"But I have thousands of followers," Natalie protested. "You want me to lose all of them?"

"Is social media a way to stay connected to the people closest to you, or it is about the endorphin rush you get from likes and shares?" Pelham asked. "I imagine that Amir is in it for the endorphins, but is that how you see social media, too? I mean, who are these followers to you?"

Natalie turned away from Pelham and shoved her phone into her back pocket. That was the first time Pelham had ever seen Natalie angry at him.

"Look, just think about it," he said softly. "If you don't want to change your settings, then don't. Just know that you have a lot of eyes watching you that also interact with Amir. It's something to consider; that's all."

Pelham spotted his and Natalie's luggage on the conveyor and stepped aside to retrieve them. After he had secured all of their bags, he glanced over to the crowd of waiting limo drivers just outside the baggage claim area. He saw one holding a sign which read, "J.P. Campbell."

"I'm J.P. Campbell," Pelham said. The limo driver approached and helped Pelham take all of the bags outside to the waiting car.

Once all of the bags were loaded into the trunk, Pelham got into the limo. Natalie was already inside, staring out the window. *She's still angry with me. I get it. Maybe I shouldn't have said anything. Some people live and die by their social media presence, but her situation is different. There are people who could use her posts against her with Amir, but she'll have to realize that on her own.*

They rode toward Bethesda in silence.

After they crossed the Potomac River, Natalie looked over at Pelham. "Sorry about the way I acted. I know you're just looking out for me."

"I shouldn't have said anything," Pelham offered.

"No, you're right. I just didn't want to hear it. Most of my followers are total strangers who watch Amir's videos. They can't be trusted. I'll start changing my privacy settings this week, so I can control who sees what and which posts can be shared."

Pelham reached for her hand. "Whatever you feel you need to do, just know that I support you."

Natalie squeezed his hand, and he saw her smile illuminated by the highway streetlights.

They pulled onto Burdette Road, Pelham's street, shortly before midnight. The road was lined on both sides with trees so thick that they created a natural canopy overhead. His home was surrounded by a high brick wall, and the long, wide driveway was blocked by a wood gate. Pelham opened the gate using a remote opener in his briefcase.

Love Lost, Love Found

As the limo pulled up to the house, motion sensors turned on hidden lights in the landscaping and the exterior lights around the house.

Natalie stared at the house when she got out of the limo. The exterior was covered in multi-colored bricks and stone, and the landscaping could best be described as lush. "What do you call this style of house?"

"French country villa," Pelham replied. "That's the look Mom and Dad were going for, and I think they pulled it off. The interior reflects that design even more."

Natalie was in awe. "This is way more beautiful than you described."

Pelham helped the limo driver remove the bags from the trunk and carry them up the stairs to the front porch. Once everything was next to the front door, Pelham signed the bill, added a generous tip for the driver, and watched the limo turn around and head back to the main road.

When the driveway gate had closed, Pelham turned toward Natalie. "Welcome to my home." He unlocked the front door and turned off the alarm. Then he and Natalie took all of the bags and placed them in the hallway at the bottom of the stairs leading to the second level.

"I can't believe how humid it is here," Natalie said as she entered the foyer. "The air's drier back in Australia."

"One of the joys of coastal living along the Atlantic Ocean," Pelham said. "You'll get used to it, but it'll play hell with your hair."

"Frizzies?" Natalie asked.

Pelham nodded.

Natalie rubbed her hair with her right hand. "Maybe it's time to give up straight hair. It does make me look young, doesn't it?"

"That's up to you," Pelham said. He looked at the luggage and then at the stairs. "Tell you what. It's late, and I'm too tired to haul all these bags upstairs to the bedroom. What do you say we leave them down here until tomorrow?"

Natalie nodded as she pivoted, so she could see the inside of his house. The floors and walls were made of the most beautiful wood Natalie had ever seen, and the Persian rugs gave the rooms she could see both warmth and class.

"Do you need anything from your luggage before we go upstairs?" Pelham asked.

Natalie held up her carry-on bag. "It's all in here."

"Then let me show you to my... our room." Pelham put his arm around her and escorted her upstairs to the master bedroom.

They were too exhausted from their long day of traveling to do anything but undress and crawl into bed. However, early the next morning, before the sun crept over the horizon, they both woke up at the same time with one thing on their mind. They made love like two people who had been apart for nearly a year, even though they hadn't left each other's side in almost a week, and when they were exhausted but satisfied, the morning sun was steaming in through the windows.

"Why don't we get cleaned up, and then I'll take you out for breakfast," Pelham suggested. "We can plan out what we're going to do today while we eat. I should buy groceries since I've been gone for so long, but I don't want to do that until we get back from our trip, so we'll be eating out this week."

"Sounds good," Natalie said.

She helped Pelham make the bed, and then he showed her around the master suite. There were two small walk-out porches overlooking the pool in the front yard opposite the driveway. The landscaping was so thick that it was impossible to see the road beyond the wall.

There were two master bathrooms, and between them was

Love Lost, Love Found

the largest walk-in closet that Natalie had ever seen. The master closet had its own washer and dryer in it, and the two bathrooms had clearly been designed for a man and a woman. The woman's bathroom had an oversized soaker tub and vanity, and the man's bathroom had a huge walk-in shower that could easily accommodate two people at the same time.

"You can use whichever bathroom you want," Pelham said. "Do you prefer tubs or showers?"

"Showers," Natalie said.

"If you'd like to shower together…"

"You read my mind."

They took full advantage of the bench in the shower to continue what they had started in the bed that morning, so it was nearly an hour later before they were cleaned and dressed. Natalie had her hair in a ponytail, and she wore a T-shirt and shorts until she could get a change of clothes from her luggage.

Pelham gave her a tour of the house, including the other bedrooms on the upper level and the main level, the office and the living room on the main level, the den, game room, and theatre in the basement, and the workout room over the secondary garage. Then he led her to the dining room on the main level and into the massive kitchen.

"I've never seen a house like this before," Natalie said, in awe of Pelham's home. "I absolutely adore it!"

"My parents spared no expense to make this their retirement paradise," Pelham said. "It's a shame they didn't get to live in it for very long."

"It looks like a perfect place for entertaining," she commented.

"It is," Pelham acknowledged. "I host several parties and gatherings here every year. I even host business retreats here for the team at least once a year, so we can get out of the office for a while."

Pelham gestured for her to follow him back to the stairs,

where their luggage was still waiting for them. "Let's take these upstairs," he suggested.

"When am I moving into the corporate apartment?" Natalie asked.

Pelham replied, "Not until at least Wednesday, although we can wait until after we get back from our trip if you want. I thought we'd go shopping today and tomorrow, so you're ready for our next trips. We need to stop by the office later in the week to introduce you to everyone and pick up the keys to your apartment, and then we can see about getting you a car, insurance, and a valid driver's license from the Motor Vehicle Administration that you can use around here."

"So, I don't actually start work until we're in New York next week?"

"Right. This week is to help you get settled and prepared for the three cities we'll be visiting."

"Then I'd love to stay here until we get back," Natalie confirmed, "If you're sure that you're okay with that."

"I'm sure," Pelham said.

Pelham helped Natalie take her luggage upstairs and put it in the walk-in closet. Then he brought his own luggage upstairs. Pelham pulled out the clothes that needed to go to the cleaners, and then he got dressed.

Natalie dressed quickly, choosing to wear the same short dress and sandals she had worn on the first day that Pelham had met her. "I'll be more comfortable in this if it's a scorcher today, and it'll be easier to take this off and put it back on when I'm trying on new clothes," she explained.

Pelham led her downstairs to the garage. There were two vehicles parked in the main garage: a sedan, and an SUV.

"The SUV is for weekends and road trips," Pelham said. "The sedan is for the city and work."

They got into the large sedan and were soon heading to the cleaners, so Pelham could drop off his clothes before heading for breakfast.

As they drive to the restaurant, Pelham called to the office. "Lauren? It's Pelham. How's everything going? Good. I got in around midnight last night. Anything that needs my immediate attention? Okay, email that to me and I'll take care of it. Today? No, I'm taking our new intern to buy clothes that look more American. I'll bring her to the office Wednesday or Thursday, and I'll need to pick up the keys to her corporate apartment then. Yes, the guesthouse. I'll help her get a car, insurance, and her license this week, too, so I won't be in much before heading to New York this weekend. Is her reservation confirmed, too? Good. Adjoining rooms? That's okay. All right, call me or text me if you need anything. Thanks, Lauren."

"She asked where I was staying?" Natalie asked.

Pelham nodded. "She likes to know everything that's going on. I felt it better to head off any gossip that might get started."

"Thanks."

At breakfast, Pelham showed Natalie a map of the area so she'd know where they were going. There were a number of clothing shops in Bethesda and Columbia, and if they couldn't find what they needed there, Pelham knew of some places in the Tysons Corner area of Northern Virginia.

"I appreciate all that you're doing for me this week, Pelham," Natalie said after breakfast, as they headed to the first clothing store. "Would you be doing all of this for me if I were any other intern?"

"If you were an intern that I had interviewed and tested like I tested you, then yes. If not, I'd probably have one of the staff or Lauren handle it."

"So, I'm not getting any special treatment."

Pelham laughed. "Well, I wouldn't let any other intern stay with me in my house, share my bed, shower with me in my bathroom, so I'd say that you are getting *some* special treatment, wouldn't you?"

Natalie giggled. "Well, if you put it that way..." Then she said, "It's going to be hard to move into the apartment. I'm getting very used to being with you every night."

"I know. For me, too. But we'll have all that figured out by the time we get back from our trip."

There was an upscale shopping village in Bethesda that catered to professionals. Pelham took Natalie there first. As he pulled into a parking space, Natalie noticed a hair salon nearby.

"Can I go there first?" she asked. "I definitely need an older look, and it will be easier to choose clothes once I know what my hair will look like."

"Good idea," Pelham said. He walked her to the salon and got her on the waiting list. "Do you want me to stay with you, or do you want to do this all on your own?"

"I want you to sit with me until they call my name," Natalie said. "I want to look at photos and get your opinion. But once the stylist starts working on me, I don't want you to see me until I have the finished look ready to unveil."

Pelham laughed. "I understand. No worries. That'll give me time to get some work done for Lauren."

They took a seat in the waiting area, and Natalie reached for the style books, so she could choose a new look. Pelham looked at each of the photos she showed him.

"Are you looking to cut your hair short, or are you looking for a style that will let you keep your hair long?" he asked.

"Long, I guess."

"Then why not look at styles that won't take a long time to fix every morning. Right now, all you have to do is brush your hair and you're ready to go. You don't want a style that'll add an extra hour to your morning routine, so find something that will frame your face beautifully, allow your hair to stay long, and won't take forever to style every day. That's my suggestion."

Natalie nodded. Then she pulled her hair back in her hand. "Do you like my hair pulled back like this?"

"That's how it looks when you wear a ponytail," Pelham noted. "I think it makes your face look lovely."

Natalie beamed. "So, any style where it's pulled back should be okay?"

Pelham nodded. "Unless the stylist recommends a different approach. Don't be afraid to try something new, as long as you trust her opinion."

The salon receptionist called Natalie's name. "Wish me luck," Natalie said as she stood.

A moment later, the reception had whisked Natalie away to meet with her stylist. Pelham pulled out his phone and began returning emails.

Natalie arrived at the station of her stylist, a girl named Sarah who looked nearly thirty and had beautiful, dark brunette hair. Sarah gestured for her to take a seat.

"Thank you," Natalie said.

"What a beautiful accent," Sarah said. "Australian?"

Natalie nodded.

"What brings you to the States?"

"A new job."

"Ah, and you need a new look for this new job?"

Natalie nodded. "Something that makes me look older and more professional, but not stuffy. And nothing that will take a lot of time to put in place every morning."

"Do you want your hair long or short?"

"Long. You can shorten it a bit, but I prefer long hair."

Sarah nodded, looking at Natalie's hair and face closely. Then she pulled out a brush to get a better idea of Natalie's hair length and thickness.

"You have such lovely hair, and your face and long neck will turn heads. Do you want to keep your eyebrows as thick as you have them or thin them out a bit?"

"What do you suggest?" Natalie asked.

"Let's see what style you choose, and then we can see what works best. Do you want to keep parting the hair in the center, to the side, or have it pulled straight back?"

"I like the part, but whatever looks best," Natalie replied.

Sarah reached for her tablet and searched for hairstyles for a minute. Then she showed a style to Natalie. "What do you think about this one? You can see that the model's hair length and thickness is similar to yours, although not feathered like yours is, it works with a part, and the way it's tucked up in the back is so easy. It shouldn't take much more than five to ten minutes each morning, and I have some accessories up front that will make it go even faster."

Natalie liked the style, and as she scrolled down, she saw two variations that she liked just as much. "Are these two just as easy?"

Sarah nodded. "Definitely. I can teach you how to do all three of them in less than thirty minutes. Then I'll let you try it until it becomes comfortable for you."

"What do you call these styles?" Natalie asked.

"They're all updos. This one is a French Twist, the second one is called a Low Bun, and the third one is called a Chignon. There are dozens of variations of each, depending on your mood or the look you want, and once you learn the basics, creating the variations is easy." Sarah showed Natalie another image. "This is called a Crossed Bun. It's chic and it keeps the hair closer to the neck, rather than having the bun stick out. It's a little trickier to learn, but it's a great look—especially for someone with your straight hair."

"I want that one," Natalie said.

Sarah smiled. "Okay. I'll teach you how to do it and let you practice it with the other three. If you've never done updos by yourself, I suggest recording the steps so you can play it back

Love Lost, Love Found

until it becomes second nature."

They discussed how Sarah wanted to cut Natalie's hair to make the styles easier to manage. Sarah also convinced Natalie to thin her thick eyebrows a little bit, and she recommended a different manicure and pedicure than the ones Natalie currently had. Natalie agreed, and Sarah went to work creating Natalie's new look.

Between the haircut, eyebrow reshaping, manicure and pedicure, and training Natalie how to style her hair to achieve the four looks that she liked, Natalie was with Sarah and her team for almost two hours.

When Natalie reappeared, wearing a near-perfect Crossed Bun hairstyle that she had styled herself, she looked older, poised, and very professional. She paid for the haircare products she'd need, the accessories to help get the hair into place each morning, and the services that the salon had provided. It wasn't cheap, but Natalie felt it was money well-spent.

Looking at herself in the full-length mirror at the front of the store, Natalie understood why Pelham had commented that her clothes made her look young. The dress she was wearing didn't match the hair style, even though it still showed off her amazing figure. *I can still wear this outfit when my hair is down on weekends, but I definitely need to wear different clothes when my hair is up like this.*

Natalie sat next to Pelham, who was busy typing an email. She gave him a gentle nudge. He looked up and didn't recognize her at first. But then his eyes went wide. "Natalie? You look incredible!"

Natalie turned her head so he could see the back.

"That's perfect," Pelham admired.

"And now I know to look for clothes that match this look," she said. "Are you ready to go?"

"Give me one minute to finish this email, and I will be."

Pelham had been working on an email to his attorney to

discuss Amir's videos of Natalie on his video channel. He typed a few more sentences, sent the email, and then he put his phone in his pocket. "Ready?"

Natalie stood. "Ready."

For the rest of the day and most of the next, Natalie shopped for clothes that complimented her new look and her figure. She purchased several skirts, slacks, and dresses for work, along with blouses and blazers. She purchased outfits that she could wear for after-work functions and nights on the town, and she also purchased casual clothes that would help her fit into the area more easily. This included swimsuits, exercise clothes, shorts, skirts, jeans, slacks, shirts, shoes and underwear. She hated how much she was spending, but she knew it was necessary if she wanted to blend in professionally and socially.

Pelham was patient with her as she tried outfit after outfit, asking his opinions about most of them. Apart from her long legs, it was easy to find clothes that fit, but harder to find clothes that created the image she wanted, while being comfortable.

"Is there anything I'm missing for our trip?" she asked toward the end of the second day.

Pelham shook his head. "You've got everything you need for the work sessions, evenings, weekends, and for some things we'll be doing in Orlando, since we have a few extra days down there to be tourists."

"So, what's next?"

"Next, we get you a Maryland driver's license, go by the office to meet your new co-workers, and then start looking for a car and teaching you to drive around the area."

"It's going to take a while to get used to driving on the wrong... the other side of the road," Natalie commented. "I've been driving on the left for eight years. That's a lot to unlearn."

Love Lost, Love Found

"I have faith in you," Pelham said.

Natalie gave him a kiss on the cheek. "Thanks again for being with me these past two days. I can't imagine doing this on my own."

"I promise you this, Natalie. You'll never have to do things alone as long as I'm around."

Natalie snuggled close to him as they walked to his car.

CHAPTER 8

Tuesday afternoon, after Natalie had finished most of her shopping, Pelham drove her back to his home, so she could put away all of her purchases. There was plenty of room in the walk-in closet for her things.

Once she had everything hung up, she set up her laptop, so she could have a video chat with her parents. Brisbane is fourteen hours ahead of Maryland, so her parents were just finishing breakfast.

While Natalie chatted with her family and showed them her new look, Pelham went into his office to call his attorney.

"Hi, Bob," he said when his attorney came on the line. Bob Prescott has been Pelham's lawyer and friend since before his parents had died.

"Hi, Pelham. What's up?"

"Did you get my email?"

"I did. I've only taken a cursory look at the issue, but I think I have good news for you."

"What?"

"The key here is the monetization of the video channel. That means that all of the content is being used for commercial purposes. It's arguable whether or not you can use someone's likeness without permission, as long as it's for private purposes, but the moment it becomes part of a commercial venture, the rules change. Positive written consent must be obtained and retained on file to use someone's likeness for a commercial venture, and that's what his video channel has become. Permissions can't be grandfathered or handled once per person. If each video is a separate commercial property, then permission is required for each and every one. Some countries, like Australia, may not enforce that rule, but she's in America now, on an Immigration visa, making her subject to and protected by United States law. Given that the company hosting Amir Dimitrios' video channel is based in the United States, that makes U.S. laws enforceable. I think we can force all content containing Natalie Patterson's likeness to be removed."

"Outstanding," Pelham said. "Can you prepare the paperwork to force the hosting company to remove the content? I don't want it filed, but I want it ready to file at a moment's notice."

"Are you expecting more trouble from this Amir fellow?" Bob asked.

"Yes. He's obsessed, he's deranged, and he'll never let Natalie go without a fight."

"Yes," Bob agreed. "I watched several of their videos, including the ones you sent of him mobilizing his fans to find her, and her rebuttal. That was very well done, by the way. I can see that he's not the type to simply go away quietly. All right. I'll get all the Cease-and-Desist letters and the legal motions drafted and ready to file. In the meantime, if anything happens, be sure to let me know."

"I will. Thanks, Bob."

"Goodnight, Pelham."

Pelham hung up the phone and saw Natalie standing in the office doorway.

"Talking to your lawyer about Amir?" she asked, taking a

seat across from his desk.

"Pelham nodded. "Fortune favors the prepared."

"Does your attorney think we can have the videos taken down?"

"Yes. Now that the channel is monetized, that makes it a commercial venture, and different laws apply. He thinks we have a very strong case."

"And he's going to get the paperwork ready for when or if we need it?"

"Right. I hope you're okay that I'm moving on this so quickly. It's better to have everything ready now. That way, if Amir ever tries something again, we can hit him where it hurts the most before he sees it coming."

Natalie smiled. "I appreciate you handling that for me. My parents said 'Hi,' and they love my new look, by the way. Now, I'm hungry. What are we going to do for dinner?"

"We can go out or we can order in," Pelham said.

"Pizza?"

"Of course. How do you like it?"

Natalie listed her favorite pizza toppings and styles.

"There's a local pizzeria about ten minutes from here that makes the best pizza in the area. How about I order from there and have it delivered?"

"Perfect."

Wednesday morning, Natalie fixed her hair into a Crossed Bun and put on one of her new office outfits—a skirt, blouse, and medium high heels that made her legs look amazing. After breakfast, Pelham was taking her to the office to introduce her to everyone, and she wanted to look her best. She also wanted to look good for her driver's license photo, since their next stop after the office was the Motor Vehicle Administration.

Love Lost, Love Found

She came downstairs and found Pelham in the kitchen, making a pot of tea.

"Can you pour me a mug?" she asked.

Pelham turned, saw what she was wearing, and stopped and smiled. "You look stunning! Good choice."

Natalie turned around slowly so he could get a better look at her. "Good enough for the office?"

"Good enough to make the women jealous and the men lecherous," Pelham confirmed.

Pelham poured her a mug of tea. "Anything new on the social media front?"

"Amir took down his original video asking his fans for help finding me. But he's still insisting that I take down my video."

"Are you going to?"

"No. Not for a while. I want him to feel helpless, like he made me feel... for a while longer."

Pelham nodded. "Hungry?"

"Starving."

"There's a diner across from The Carriage House. How about eating there?"

"The Carriage House?"

"That's the name of the building where the office is located," Pelham explained. "The architectural style is that of an old English or Colonial barn where coaches and carriages were kept when not in use. I took one look at it and knew that I wanted it for my company."

"You own it?" Natalie asked as she finished her tea.

Pelham nodded. "Technically, the firm owns it, but I made arrangements for its purchase and the reconfiguration of the interior. There's enough room for me to more than double the staff before having to restructure anything, and the location is perfect. You'll see what I mean when we get there."

Pelham picked up her empty mug. "Want a refill, or are you ready to go?"

"I'm ready to go." She grabbed her purse as they headed for the garage. Natalie was used to carrying her identification and credit cards in her pockets, but she felt like she needed something classier for the office. While shopping for clothes, she had found a deep red leather shoulder bag that wasn't much larger than the average paperback novel. It had a matching wallet and business card case, and it could also hold her phone, keys, and a few personal items. She loved the size and the look.

"How far is the office?" Natalie asked as they pulled out of the driveway.

"About ten minutes, depending on traffic," Pelham answered.

Traffic was light that morning, and seven minutes later, Natalie saw a beautiful building on the right side of the street. The name *Mason, Campbell, Alvarado, & Jürgen, LLP* was on the sign above the door. "You're right. The building is lovely," she said as Pelham turned left into the diner's parking lot.

Natalie felt the humidity as soon as she got out of the car. *I'm glad this hairdo helps prevent frizzies.*

They took one of the tables near the windows. "The staff should start arriving in the next fifteen minutes, so everyone will be there by the time we finish breakfast," Pelham said.

They ordered their food.

"I can't get over how great you look in that outfit," Pelham commented. "You wear it like you've always dressed like that."

Natalie beamed. "I can't believe how comfortable it is. I always thought work clothes would be confining in all the wrong places, but this outfit feels as relaxing as the little dress I wore the first day we went shopping. And the more I wear heels, the more I enjoy wearing them. I always had spiked heels for nights on the town, but I wore flats during the day. These shoes feel great, and I feel powerful wearing them."

Pelham laughed. "You're the first woman I've ever met who said that a pair of heeled shoes were comfortable. They must be really good."

A few minutes later, their food arrived. Natalie watched the parking lot across the street at the Carriage House and saw Pelham's staff start arriving.

"How many people work out of your office?" she asked.

"Eleven, including me. Twelve now that you're here."

She pointed toward the office with her fork. "Then you and I are the only ones not there already."

Pelham nodded and pulled out his phone. After he dialed the number, he said, "Lauren? Good morning. We're across the street having breakfast." Pelham glanced at Natalie's plate. "We'll be there in about ten minutes. Can you round up everyone and tell them we're meeting in the conference room in fifteen? Perfect. See you shortly. Bye."

Pelham put his phone away and looked at Natalie. "Are you ready to meet everyone?"

Natalie was feeling a bit nervous, but she was also excited. "I am."

He gestured toward her plate. "Do you need anything else? A refill?"

Natalie shook her head. "No, thanks. I'm done. Thanks for breakfast."

Pelham smiled. "My pleasure."

Pelham paid the check, and then he and Natalie got back into his car. Crossing the street wasn't easy, given the lack of traffic lights on that stretch of road, but they made it to the Carriage House parking lot a few minutes later.

When Pelham pulled into an open parking space, Natalie asked, "You don't have your own parking spot? I thought partners would always have reserved parking."

"It didn't feel right," Pelham replied. "I may run the office, but the staff does the work for our clients. I want to make certain that they get the perks, not me. Now, when I worked on Madison Avenue in New York, the partners had their own floor of the parking deck. I swore I'd never be like that, and I've held to that promise."

He puts his people first. I'm glad he treats everyone that way and not just me. I'm impressed. She got out of the car and followed him inside the office.

Lauren was waiting for them in the foyer. "Good morning, Boss," she said when he entered the building. Turning to Natalie, she said, "And you must be Natalie. Welcome! If you need anything, just ask me."

"Pleased to meet you," Natalie said.

"Lauren is our Office Manager," Pelham told her. "She also coordinates with payroll, accounting, human resources, she orders all the office supplies, arranges travel… basically everything needed to keep the office running. I couldn't get anything done without her."

Lauren blushed at the compliment. "They're all waiting in the conference room."

"Tell them I'll be there in a few moments."

Lauren nodded and headed down the hallway. It was not lost on Natalie that Lauren's casual glance was actually a quick appraisal of Natalie's appearance, as if Lauren were trying to figure out if there were something going on between Natalie and Pelham. Natalie smiled and followed Pelham to the conference room.

There were ten people sitting around the large conference table: four men and six women.

"Good morning everyone," Pelham said as he entered the room. "I brought someone back from Australia—our new intern, Natalie Patterson."

Everyone said hello to Natalie.

Pelham then went around the table. "You've met Lauren O'Donovan already. To her left are the two people responsible for sales—Daniel Shaw, and Richard Oliver."

Pelham gestured to the other people seated at the table.

"The rest of these folks handle brand management and publicist services." Then he introduced Brent Kelley, Melanie Brown, Luisa Cruz, Briana Knowles, Luke Reed, Rose Skye, and Nadine Richardson.

He gestured for Natalie to sit, and he sat at the head of the table. "Natalie, why don't you tell everyone a little about yourself."

"Well, I was born in Brisbane, Australia, which is the capital of Queensland on the east coast," Natalie began. "I lived there most of my life. I attended uni at the University of Queensland and graduated with a Business Management/Commerce degree, majoring in International Business. I saw the posting for the firm's internship program, and it sounded like a great way to put my degree to use, so I applied, and after a few twists and turns, I was accepted. I was raised driving on the left side of the road, so I apologize in advance if my driving terrorizes anyone while I try to get used to doing everything backwards. Also, it has been pointed out to me that I use a fair bit of Australian slang out of habit, so if you don't understand what I'm saying, please ask. It'll help me identify the slang I don't even think about and start using words that make more sense around here."

Natalie looked around the room, and she immediately understood what Pelham had told her that morning. The women looked slightly jealous of her youthful looks, and the men all seemed mesmerized by her accent. She resisted the urge to giggle.

"What did you do for fun back home?" Richard Oliver from sales asked.

"I'm a runner," Natalie responded, "and I do yoga. Queensland is an outdoorsman's paradise, so I also went hiking a lot. We have the best beaches in Australia, so I went to the coast with my mates every chance I could. I also love to travel. I've been to Ireland—where my father's from—South Korea, Japan,

New Zealand, and now the United States."

After Richard broke the ice, everyone started asking questions—some to know more about her and some just to hear her talk.

"Where are you living?" Briana Knowles asked.

"The firm arranged a corporate apartment for me just down the street," Natalie replied. "All I need now is a car, and I'm all set."

Natalie saw Lauren flash a look at Pelham, but she didn't say anything.

"How does the weather compare with home?" Rose Skye asked.

"Well, we just finished summer back home, and it's fall now. The leaves were turning when I left. Now I'm back in spring, it's more humid than I thought it would be, and I'll be facing another summer followed by a real winter, which we don't really get in Brisbane or Sydney. I think I'm in for quite a shock living in Maryland."

"When are you starting here at the office?" Brent Kelley asked.

"I'm traveling to New York, Orlando, and Chicago with the boss over the next three weeks, so I'll start working out of this office when we return from that trip."

"Speaking of which," Pelham interjected. "I need to show Natalie where her workspace is, and then she has some paperwork to sign."

He stood, signaling that the meeting was over. Everyone welcomed Natalie to the firm and filed out of the conference room.

"I have the paperwork ready," Lauren said. "I'll bring it to your office after you show Natalie around."

Pelham nodded and escorted Natalie down the hall.

"Everyone here gets an individual office," Pelham explained as he showed her around the building. "Yours will be in between Nadine's and Briana's. Nadine is our best publicist, and you'll be working closely with her when we get back from Chicago. Once you've learned everything she can teach you, I'll pair you up with Briana, who's one of our best brand managers. Between the two of them, you should learn everything you need to know to be successful at delivering either of those services."

Natalie nodded. She was thrilled when she saw her office. In addition to the desk, chairs, and credenza, she had two whiteboards and several filing cabinets. She even had a new computer with multiple monitors already set up.

"All computers are hooked to networked printers, which are located three doors down from your office, next to the break room." Pelham then showed her the break room, and where the supplies and other equipment were located.

Pelham led Natalie to his office, which was just past Laurens' on the other side of the building's entrance. It was considerably larger than the other offices, having its own sofa and matching chairs, coffee table, and conference table.

Natalie sat down at the conference table, and Lauren knocked on the door.

"Come in," Pelham said.

Lauren joined Natalie at the conference table. Pelham sat at his desk so he could check messages and read his mail.

"Here's your lease for the corporate apartment," Lauren said. "Be sure to take this to the MVA as proof of residency."

Natalie signed the original lease—that Lauren would keep on file—and the copy, that Natalie would keep. Then Lauren explained all of the new hire paperwork. Natalie signed the employment agreement, the confidentiality agreement, and the personnel forms required by HR. She also completed the direct deposit information form for Payroll. *I'm glad I already confirmed that my account at Pelham's bank is active and that the wire of all my money from Australia has already posted. I still need to get a credit card, but I guess the debit card will work for now.*

Next, Lauren went through the IRS and INS forms. Natalie handed over her Australian passport so Lauren could make a copy of Natalie's visa and the other paperwork she'd received from the U.S. Consulate in Sydney. Once all of the paperwork had been signed and the credentials verified, Lauren took the paperwork, made copies for Natalie, and scanned the forms to send to the Internship Coordinator at the main office. The originals would be stored in Pelham's files.

"Is there anything else you need from me, Boss?" Lauren asked as she put Natalie's file in Pelham's staff filing cabinet.

"Just last month's financials and the month-to-date numbers for this month," Pelham said. "You can email them to me. I want to look over things tonight."

"I'll do that right now," Lauren promised. Glancing at the clock on the wall, she added, "Don't forget what the MVA is like in the mornings."

"Right." Pelham stood. "We should head over there. Thanks, Lauren!"

Natalie stood. "Thanks, Lauren," she said, picking up the envelope of paperwork that Lauren had given her. "Is there anything else I need?"

Lauren slapped her forehead. "Yes. I need to make your badge and give you your entry card and the keys to your office. Come with me."

Natalie followed Lauren to her office. In the corner was a machine to take photographs and print them onto laminated badges. Lauren showed Natalie where to sit, and then she turned on the machine, took Natalie's photo, and printed the photo on Natalie's badge.

While the badge was printing, Lauren obtained an entry card that served as an electronic key needed to enter the building after hours. She placed it into a device, encoded it with a four-digit code that Natalie selected, and activated it to work with the building's security system. Lauren removed it and placed it onto a lanyard. She then checked the printed badge and placed it on the same lanyard in front of the entry card.

She crossed the room to another filing cabinet and retrieved a set of keys that would unlock Natalie's office door, desk, credenza, and filing cabinets. After Natalie verified that the keys worked, Lauren told Pelham that Natalie was all set.

"Thanks, Lauren. We'll chat tomorrow, and then I'll see you after we return from Chicago."

"Have a safe trip, Boss."

Pelham and Natalie arrived at the MVA and found that it was already crowded. Natalie checked in at the desk to get a number, and then she started filling out all the paperwork that was required. Once her number was called, she was directed to the person who would be handling her request. An hour later, Natalie walked out of the MVA with her new Maryland driver's license.

"I'm surprised they let you keep your Australian license," Pelham commented.

"They said I'll have to surrender it if I become a permanent resident, but since there's the chance that I'll have to go back to Australia after the internship is over, they let me keep it."

"I hope you won't go back if you're not offered a permanent position with the firm," Pelham said as they walked to the car. "I want you to stay here... with me."

Natalie stopped and looked at him. "Are you sure about that? A lot can change in a year. Hell, a lot can change in a week. Look at all that's happened to me."

"Well, barring something completely unforeseen happening, I know I don't ever want to lose you. I happen to love you."

Natalie's eyes went wide. "You... love me? Actually?"

Pelham nodded and put his arms around her. "We've spent every day together for the past month. I could date someone the traditional way for a year and not spend that much time with her. Every minute we're together convinces me more that you're the only one I want to be with. If you don't get a job offer at the end of the internship, I'll do whatever is necessary to keep you here with me, if that's what you want, too."

Natalie looked into his eyes. "I don't know what will happen tomorrow, let alone a year from now. But I love you, too. You're the apple of my eye, my man, and I want to spend the rest of my life with you. I don't want that to ever change. You're the finest, the best man I've ever known, and you're the only man who has ever made me feel special. And if this all ends tomorrow, I want you to know the last month has been the best days of my life. I mean that."

She leaned in, and Pelham kissed her deeply. They held the embrace for a while, until they realized that everyone coming in and out of the MVA could see them.

"What other errands do we have for today?" Natalie whispered.

"None that can't wait until tomorrow."

"Then let's go home. I need to be with you right now, and it's a bit too public around here."

Pelham nodded and walked her to the car. He set speed records driving back to his house.

CHAPTER 9

When they arrived at Pelham's house, and the car was parked in the garage, Natalie wasted no time jumping out and running up the stairs to Pelham's bedroom. Pelham raced after her, stopping off in the kitchen just long enough to grab a couple of water bottles.

When he entered the bedroom, he didn't see Natalie anywhere. "Where are you?" he called out.

"Be there in a minute," she answered. Her voice was coming from the closet.

"Need any help in there?"

"No, thank you. Just adjust the curtains and get your clothes off."

Pelham put the water bottles on the night tables and closed the curtains so no light would come in through three of the windows, but he left the curtains on the fourth window slightly open so there'd be enough light to see. He preferred to sleep in the dark, but when he made love to Natalie, he liked a little light to see her response to whatever he was doing.

Once the light was just right, he undressed and laid his clothes on one of the chairs between the windows facing the bed. Then he crawled between the sheets, waiting for Natalie.

She appeared a moment later, wearing a midnight blue silk slip that would have to be called a shirt if it were any shorter. She spun around so Pelham could see that it was practically backless—only the crisscrossing shoulder straps covered the beautiful tanned skin of her back. The slip provided minimal coverage, and with the high slits on the side showing off Natalie's amazing legs, Pelham was immediately aroused.

"Like it?" she purred as she let her hair down and shook it.

"I love it," Pelham responded. "I'd love it even more if you were over here."

Natalie crossed the room, crawled onto the bed, pulled the covers down, and straddled Pelham. "Better?" she asked.

Pelham reached up and let his hands run from her breasts down and around to her shapely behind. "You're getting there."

Natalie lifted off the slip and let it fall to the floor. "How about now?"

Pelham pulled her down so their lips could meet. "Perfect," he whispered, kissing her deeply.

Natalie felt his arousal and began rubbing herself against him as they kissed.

At first, Pelham's hands explored the sensitive parts of her breasts, but as her rubbing intensified, he reached around and clutched her glutes.

They both began moaning, and Natalie moved down to let her tongue and mouth continue stimulating Pelham's growing manhood. Soon, Pelham's head was pressed into the pillows as the sensations Natalie was causing coursed through his body.

After several minutes, he whispered, "Spin around."

She complied, and soon their tongues and mouths were pleasing each other at the same time. Natalie had never done this before, but she found the sensations of giving and receiving pleasure at the same time mind-blowing. Soon, she was climaxing uncontrollably as she continued pleasing Pelham. When she began climaxing again, she felt Pelham swell rapidly, signaling that his release was about to explode. She tightened her lips and increased speed. Pelham let out a long, deep moan, and Natalie felt and tasted him climax. She continued moving her head up and down rapidly, and he continued climaxing.

When he had finished, he was still fully erect. Natalie spun around and guided him in so he was penetrating her. She moved up and down on him, and soon they were both moaning as the sensations from their connection intensified.

Natalie's stomach muscles began spasming, and her legs muscles quivered as the next climax hit her. She was panting, and her skin glistened as she continued moving up and down on him.

Pelham rolled her off and onto her knees. He penetrated her from behind, driving deeply and causing her to moan with each thrust. He kept his hands on her waist, holding on to her so his penetrations went even deeper. Suddenly, she began bucking as she was hit with her most intense orgasm yet. Pelham held onto her as her legs lost control, quivering irrepressibly.

A few minutes later, another intense orgasm hit her the same way, and once the climax had passed, Pelham rolled Natalie over onto her back and lay on top of her, kissing her and feeling the sweat on her breasts pressing against his chest. Natalie reached down and guided him inside. Then she wrapped her long, lean legs around him, holding him close with her legs and arms as they kissed. He began thrusting while they kissed, and Natalie continued holding him as close as she could.

Pelham felt her shaking, and when he slowed down, she whispered, "Don't. Don't stop."

Pelham obliged and increased speed again. He felt her climax several more times, but she wouldn't release him from her embrace, and she wouldn't let him slow or break the connection. He felt his own release building, so he deepened his thrusts, increasing speed.

Natalie gasped as an intense climax hit, causing her whole

body to shake. Only embracing Pelham so tightly kept her on the bed. The muscles inside of her clenched, and the sensation pushed Pelham over the edge. He released, and she squealed with delight when she felt the hot liquid shooting deep inside of her. Soon, Pelham was completely drained, and he and Natalie continued holding onto each other, enjoying the aftermath of what they had just shared.

When Natalie unclenched her legs, Pelham rolled over, pulling Natalie on top of him. She stretched out with her arms around him and her legs straddling him.

"That. Was. Incredible!" she whispered into his ear.

"I have no words," Pelham agreed.

"I can't move. I'm afraid to even try."

"Then don't," Pelham said softly. He held her tightly. "Just relax and enjoy the moment."

She stayed on top of him for several minutes, then she slid off and lay next to him, with her legs intertwined with his, her head on his shoulder, and her arm around his chest. "It's astonishing how you make me feel inside, outside, all over. When I'm making love to you, it's not just physical. It's... I can't even describe it. It's like you're not just loving my body, you're loving all of me at the same time. It's incredible."

"I've never loved being with any woman the way I love being with you," Pelham said. "I'd always heard the expression that two become one when making love, and I understood the physical connection you have during sex, but now I understand that there's so much more going on than just the physical aspects when two people truly love each other. I finally understand how cheap and unfulfilling casual sex can be. After you've had what we've just shared, nothing else can ever be good enough."

"Too right," Natalie agreed. "That's how I know that Amir and I never once made love. It was just about him having a naughty with me—just a way to get his tackle inside my pink bits—and if I got to enjoy any of it, too, well, bloody good for

Love Lost, Love Found

me. That was never part of his plan—an afterthought, if that."

Pelham tried not to laugh. "The naughty? Tackle and pink bits?"

Natalie blushed. "Australian slang, sorry. *Anyway,* what I'm trying to say is that the difference between what he and I shared and what you and I share is like comparing a shack to a palace."

"I'm the palace, right?"

Natalie pinched his chest gently. "Of course you're the palace. You're ten palaces."

Pelham leaned down and kissed her. "And I promise I always will be, as long as you let me."

"That'll be forever," Natalie purred.

After a few minutes, she propped herself up on her elbow, so she could look Pelham in his eyes. "Do you forgive me for talking about Amir? I know it's wrong to talk about a former… relationship, especially after what we just experienced together, but after four years under his control, I still compare everything new I'm experiencing with the way things were with him, and I see just how little I knew about real love. I don't know any other way to express it, other than to compare you to him. If it's weird or rude, let me know."

Pelham smiled. "I understand. It's hard not to compare. I admit that I've been comparing you with women from my past, too. And there is no comparison. I always felt like sex was just a transaction with them, but there was never any real… emotion, bond, or sharing with them, and I didn't know what I had been missing until I met you. And now that I know, nothing else will ever satisfy me. I'm… well… all I know is that you make me happy, and you make me want to make you happy. I can't imagine anything else ever feeling as right as this—what we have right now."

Natalie stretched up and kissed Pelham, and in that kiss, Pelham felt all the love she had for him and that he had for her. Without realizing how or when it happened, he was inside of her again, needing to be one—body, mind, and soul.

The connection was so intense that Natalie began crying. Pelham stopped and just held on to her until she had let it all out.

"I'm sorry," she said, drying her eyes. "I don't know what came over me. It was so intense that it felt like you broke through something... a wall... an emotional wall that I was keeping around my heart so I wouldn't get hurt again. And now that the wall is broken, I'm not afraid anymore. The past... it's powerless. I feel... I feel free."

Natalie kissed Pelham, and then her head moved down to stimulate his manhood so they could finish what they had started.

An hour later, they finally broke the connection. They were both sweating, and soon they had drained their water bottles, trying to replenish the liquids their bodies desperately needed.

"How are you feeling?" Pelham asked as she snuggled next to him.

"Better, thanks," Natalie said. "I've never experienced an emotional release like that before. It freaked me out. I hope it didn't freak you out."

"It did at first, but once I realized why you were crying, it made sense. I guess it's like being lost in the desert, starving and thirsty, and then suddenly being in the shade having something to eat and drink. It's a shock to the system that the emotions have to process somehow."

Natalie nodded slowly. "It was exactly like that. I hope I never go through that again, but it's good to know that I can with you, if there's ever another need."

"Whatever you need, anytime you need it," Pelham promised.

After they had showered and changed the sheets on the bed,

Love Lost, Love Found

Natalie and Pelham went downstairs to the living room to relax. Both wore only T-shirts and shorts, and Natalie's hair was pulled back into a ponytail.

"So, what are the plans for the rest of the week?" Natalie asked.

"Well, today is Wednesday, and we fly to New York Saturday morning, so you have time to see the city before the workshops and seminars begin on Monday. Even though you won't need it until we get back from our trip, I'd suggest getting your car picked out and contracted this week, so you can pick it up when we're back in town. You do need to start learning to drive the American way."

Natalie's shoulders slumped a bit. "I wish I could just live here with you." Her eyes widened and her hand flew up and covered her mouth when she realized what she had said.

Pelham grinned. "I've been thinking the same thing, but there are two very good reasons why it's too soon for that."

Curious, Natalie asked, "What reasons?"

"First, if we're going to maintain the illusion that there's nothing going on between us, you need to be seen coming and going from the office by yourself, and not at the same time as me every day. You also need to be seen heading to and from the direction of the corporate apartment."

Natalie nodded.

"And second, a wise person once told me that you're never really ready to live with someone else until you've lived alone and proven that you can make it on your own. That way, no one you're living with will have power over you because you allow yourself to become dependent on him. Once you know that you don't need to live with someone to survive, you'll never be afraid to leave a bad situation."

"There would never be a bad situation with you," Natalie stated.

"I agree, but what if something happens to me? You need

the confidence to know that you can make it on your own. Does that make sense?"

Natalie nodded. "I know you're just looking out for me, but I hate the thought of not being with you at night."

"I never said we weren't going to be together much of the time," Pelham said. "I just said that I think it's best if we maintain appearances and you keep your own place—at least until the end of the internship. After that, we'll reevaluate everything and see what works best for us. Okay?"

Natalie smiled. "Okay. As long as we spend a lot of time with each other outside the office."

Pelham agreed.

"So, what else do we need to do?" Natalie asked.

Pelham leaned back. "Well, if we get the car taken care of tomorrow, then we can drive over to Baltimore and then Annapolis so you can see the State Capital and the Chesapeake Bay. Some of the best seafood is available in the area, and it's time to introduce you to what Maryland is famous for—Crab."

Natalie loved trying new food. "Sounds great. And Friday?"

"We could drive to DC and let you see the capital," Pelham suggested.

"How far away are we from there?" Natalie asked.

"Thirty minutes, maybe forty depending on traffic."

"That close?"

Pelham nodded. "I drive down there all the time. There's great food, lots of history, and if you love architecture like I do, there's so much to see and do. If you're thinking about living in the U.S. permanently, possibly even becoming a citizen, you should really start immersing yourself in The Great Experiment."

"The great what?"

"What we call the founding of the Republic," Pelham explained. "Sustained self-governance had never been attempted successfully before, so it was an experiment to see if we could survive as a nation. We almost didn't, but we're still here."

"It sounds like fun. So, we'll do that on Friday?"

"Yes. Is there anything you want to see or do before our trip Saturday?"

Natalie shrugged. "Apart from getting a new phone, I'm not sure. I feel like there's so much."

"There is," Pelham agreed, "and we have plenty of time to do it all. That's what weekends are for."

"So I need to learn patience?"

Pelham smiled. "It'll help."

Pelham helped Natalie create an updated budget to use when looking at cars. After adding up the rent, insurance, utilities, gasoline, groceries, and other expenses, Natalie saw how much she could afford for a monthly car lease.

"What can I get for this much money?" Natalie asked.

Pelham pulled up a website where you entered your location and the amount you wanted to pay, and it showed you what cars were available. Natalie found quite a few that were within her budget.

"I thought for sure that everything would be out of my price range," she exclaimed.

"To purchase? Perhaps. To rent? Not so much. That's why we suggested a lease."

Natalie selected three dealerships that offered discounts to Pelham's firm and seven potential rentals that interested her.

Thursday morning, Natalie's hair was up in a French Twist, and she was wearing slacks, heels, and a blouse. "Most of my driving will be to and from work, so I might as well do the test drives in work clothes," she explained. "I'll change clothes on our way to Baltimore."

They left the house, arriving at the closest dealership right before it opened. This dealership had three cars that Natalie liked, including one that was a newer model of the car she'd owned in Australia, before Amir destroyed it.

When the dealership doors opened, Pelham explained that he was helping one of his new employees lease a car while she was working in the U.S. The dealer understood—it was a common scenario for that part of the country, being so close to the DC and Northern Virginia area.

After verifying what she was prepared to spend, and the firm's discount, the dealer showed Natalie the cars she had identified online the day before. He then allowed her to test drive them, which took a bit of training, since Natalie had never driven on the American side of the road before. Fortunately, the dealership had a driving track in the back where foreign nationals could learn to drive before venturing out on the public roadways.

Natalie did quite well staying on the right side of the road, but she kept looking left then right when crossing intersections, when she should be looking right then left. The only other thing she had problems with was finding where the controls were located on the steering column and the dashboard, since everything was either backward or simply in a different place.

In the end, Natalie loved the newer model of the car she had owned in Australia. If felt the most comfortable and familiar, and the price—which included insurance—was well below her budget maximum. She signed the lease, effective the Saturday after she and Pelham would return from Chicago, and the dealer promised that it would be ready to pick up that day. Natalie paid the deposit, and then she and Pelham left the dealership and headed for the cellular phone store before going to Baltimore.

Natalie lowered the passenger seat of the car, so she was

Love Lost, Love Found

almost lying flat. She removed the blouse and the slacks, and quickly pulled on a cute top and a dressy pair of shorts. Then she pulled on her runners and put her work clothes in the bag that had held her other clothes.

When she raised the back of her seat, Pelham was amazed at how fast she had changed. "Have you done that in a car before?" he asked. "It all seemed a bit... experienced."

Natalie didn't have to answer. Her face was blushing bright red. Pelham laughed and kept driving.

After getting the new phone with a local phone number, and getting her data transferred over from her old phone, they drove to Baltimore. Natalie texted the members of her family with her new number, but she didn't tell her other friends, vowing to do that over the next few weeks.

Natalie fell in love with Federal Hill, the Inner Harbor, and Little Italy in downtown Baltimore. Then they drove south, and when she saw Annapolis for the first time, she was amazed. As they took the circle around the State House, Pelham explained the building's history. Then he drove her past the United States Naval Academy on the banks of the Severn River.

Natalie kept her face against the window, trying to take in all that she was seeing.

They had lunch at a little restaurant on the southern edge of the city, between the Horn Point Harbor Marina and the Annapolis Maritime Museum and Park. The restaurant looked out over the Chesapeake Bay. Pelham introduced Natalie to Crab Cakes, which she immediately loved.

After touring the museum and the marina, Pelham drove West on US-50 to the Capital Beltway, I-495. He followed the Beltway north and then west until he reached the Bethesda exit. He turned south, and headed back to the house.

"I can't get over how different everything looks here," Natalie said as they turned into Pelham's neighborhood. "The rivers, the foliage, the terrain... it's all so different."

"I imagine that Queensland is more similar to Florida and the Caribbean Islands," Pelham said as he turned onto his street. "Semi-tropical coasts seem to look alike. The mid-Atlantic is more like northern and central Europe. Probably explains why it was so popular with immigrants from those areas."

They went to bed early that night. Pelham wanted to get an early start to avoid the worst of the DC morning commute. "I know a great place for breakfast near the Smithsonian," he said. "If we can get there early enough, then we should be able to hit most of the tourist spots before it gets too crowded."

Friday morning, Pelham drove to DC, passing the Washington National Cathedral on the way to Georgetown. He drove through DC to Pennsylvania Avenue, and then to Constitution Avenue and the National Mall.

Natalie was surprised as they drove by the iconic White House, but when she saw the Mall, with its monuments, and then the Capital Building, she trembled slightly.

"All my life, I've seen these buildings on television and in movies," Natalie said, "but I never thought I'd see them with my own eyes. And you live so close to them. I've been to Canberra before, but it's nothing like this."

Pelham drove to the restaurant. After breakfast, they drove to one of the pickup spots for the bus tours and spent the next six hours visiting the key sites that made DC such a popular place to vacation.

By the end of the day, as they drove back to Maryland, Natalie was exhausted, but happy… and loaded down with souvenirs—some for herself and some to send home to her family. "I can't thank you enough to taking me there," she said. "I know Australia and the U.S. are almost the same size—"

"If you ignore Alaska and Hawaii," Pelham interrupted.

Love Lost, Love Found

Natalie nodded. "But I think there's more to see and do here than there is back there. I could spend the rest of my life here and barely scratch the surface, right?"

"Right," Pelham confirmed. "But what a fun way to spend the rest of your life."

"With you," Natalie added.

Saturday morning, they flew to New York. Natalie was shocked at how tall the skyscrapers were, but Pelham could see that she was uneasy.

"What's wrong?"

"I feel so closed in here," she confided as the cab headed for their hotel. "I can't see the sky, and I feel so... claustrophobic. There are too many people, too many cars, and too many buildings. I'm used to everything being more spread out than this."

Pelham patted her hand. "Six million people on a tiny island is a bit much. Trust me; I know how you feel. But it's not all bad... especially lit up at night. There are always ways to enjoy a place, even one as different as New York."

Natalie looked skeptical, but she nodded and closed her eyes.

That afternoon, after they checked into their hotel, they went shopping along Fifth Avenue. Natalie enjoyed herself once she was inside the stores, but she hated having to walk on the sidewalks with so many other people.

"I just don't feel safe out there," she said when they got back to their rooms.

They had adjacent rooms at the hotel, and the food was so good there that they ordered room service for dinner. Natalie kept her things in her room, but the connecting doorway was left open, and they ate and slept in Pelham's room.

On Sunday, they planned the workshops and seminars for the week. Pelham decided to let Natalie handle as many of the sessions as she felt comfortable leading, which worked out to just over half of the sessions.

Once the workshops and seminars started, Natalie felt more comfortable leading her sessions, and she was more confident reading the room, so she knew which topics to emphasize and which didn't require as much explanation.

On Thursday afternoon, after the last session, Pelham collected the participant evaluations and shared them with Natalie. They were glowing, and Natalie received high praise from the attendees.

The next morning they flew to Orlando, Florida, and as soon as they arrived, Natalie was all smiles. "This reminds me of home," she said happily. "It's warm, everything is spread out, and there are palm trees everywhere!"

Their hotel was south of the city, near the theme parks, and they had adjacent rooms again. Once they were settled, they spent the rest of Friday and the weekend being tourists.

The workshops in Orlando went just as well as the ones in New York had. Pelham allowed Natalie to handle more of the sessions on her own, and she rose to the occasion. The participant evaluations echoed the ones from New York, praising Natalie and crediting her for making the workshops successful.

Pelham contacted Wes several times, letting him know how well Natalie was doing. "I look forward to meeting her the week after you get back from Chicago," Wes said to Pelham the night before Pelham and Natalie flew to Chicago.

When they arrived in Chicago, Pelham was happy to find that their hotel, The Chicago Marriott Downtown, had a great view of Lake Michigan from the upper floors. Natalie didn't feel as closed in as she did in New York, but she still wasn't comfortable walking along the streets of the city.

Once settled at the hotel, they took a cab up Michigan Avenue to Water Tower Place.

"What is this place?" Natalie asked.

"It's a high-rise shopping mall," Pelham answered. "It's the only one I've ever seen. It's a place everyone needs to visit when they come to Chicago."

After spending a few hours there, they took a cab to The Berghoff Restaurant. "I thought you might like to try some German food," Pelham said as they rode south.

They dined on Weiner Schnitzel, creamed spinach, and house-made spätzle, and in spite of German food being considered heavy, Natalie loved it.

The next day, they stayed at the hotel. "How do you feel about handling the entire workshop yourself?" Pelham asked.

"What will you be doing?" she asked.

"Observing you and being ready to step in if there's a question you can't answer," Pelham replied.

"So, I'd be facilitating, and you'd be interjecting your wisdom and filling in the blanks for whatever I can't answer?"

"Exactly."

"I'm game. But if I start to muck it up, you should step in before the attendees get annoyed."

"I'll do that," Pelham assured her. "I don't want to make you feel overwhelmed or risk the attendee's experience. This is marketing for us, after all."

"Okay. Let's see what happens."

Natalie handled all of the sessions that week, and Pelham only had to step in twice, when the questions being asked touched on topics that Natalie couldn't answer. Natalie called on Pelham several times to add his own experiences to the discussions, but she handled everything else. Pelham was delighted with her performance, and the attendees praised Natalie and the sessions.

Pelham and Natalie flew back to Maryland on Friday afternoon. The next morning, they picked up Natalie's new car, and Pelham followed her as she drove it to her corporate apartment. Then he drove them back to his place to pack up all of her belongings—other than a few items that she was keeping at Pelham's for when she stayed over—and move them to her apartment.

They loaded everything into his SUV and drove it to her place, which was fully furnished. Pelham helped her carry her things inside and put the clothes away. Then he took her to a local grocery store to pick up the food she'd need for the next week. She was amazed when she saw an America grocery store for the first time. "We don't get this many options back home."

Once the groceries were put away, Pelham asked her, "Do you want to come back to my place, or do you want to stay here and get used to living in your own place?"

Natalie just stared at him. "Ummm... both? I want to get used to being in my own place, but I don't want to wait until Monday to see you again."

"Well, while you make up your mind, I have something for you. It's in the car. I'll be right back."

"What is it?" she asked as he headed for the door.

"Just a little something you'll need for next week."

He stepped out and returned a minute later with an oversized gift bag. He handed it to her.

She opened it and found it contained a soft-side briefcase like the one Pelham carried. It had the firm's name stitched on

Love Lost, Love Found

it—Mason, Campbell, Alvarado, & Jürgen, LLP—and the firm's logo.

"Now you look like someone who works for the firm," he said as she looked at it.

"Thank you!" Natalie threw her arms around his neck and hugged him tightly. "I love it."

Natalie pulled away and looked intently at Pelham. "Are you in a hurry to leave?" she asked.

"There's nowhere else I'd rather be," he replied. "Why?"

"I thought you'd like to help me christen the place." She gestured toward the bedroom.

Pelham smiled. Then he locked the front door, picked her up, and carried her into the next room.

Chapter 10

Monday morning, Pelham pulled into the parking lot of the Carriage House. He recognized Wes' car immediately. *He drove three-and-a-half hours from Pittsburgh rather than flying down? He'd normally consider that a poor use of time that could be better spent working with clients. I guess he would've wasted time in the airports, but he has to drive all the way back. I love my car, too, but geez!*

When Pelham entered the building, he heard Wes talking to Lauren O'Donovan and Daniel Shaw, who were usually the first two in the office every day. He followed their voices and found them in the break room, getting coffee.

"Hi, Wes!" he said. "Long drive?"

"Hi, Pelham," Wes responded. "Yeah, but it's relaxing. Beverly chose to fly, so she'll be here in a couple of hours."

"How long are you staying?" Pelham asked.

"I'm driving home later today, and Beverly is flying out this afternoon." Wes gestured toward the door, and the two of them headed for Pelham's office. "I have a few ideas I want to run past you before everyone gets here. I also want to meet Natalie, and then I'll meet with the rest of the team."

"Okay." Pelham had known that Wes was coming down

Love Lost, Love Found

that week, but for the boss to be waiting for him on a Monday morning with no advanced notice made Pelham apprehensive. He unlocked his office door, allowed Wes to enter, and then closed the door behind them. Wes took a seat at the conference table and motioned for Pelham to join him.

"Relax, Pelham," Wes said, looking at Pelham's expression. "There's nothing wrong. In fact, everything is great. But I wanted to talk to you about Natalie before I talk to her."

"Okay, shoot."

"How are things between you two?" Wes asked.

"Progressing," Pelham answered cautiously.

Wes grinned. "Will you relax? I said that everything's great. I just need some information to help me pick from a couple of options running through my head."

"All right. What specifically do you want to know?"

"How far has your relationship progressed?"

"Pretty far," Pelham admitted. "Yesterday is the first day we've been apart since we met, and the first time we didn't stay together at night since our last week in Sydney."

"So, it's serious?"

"And getting more serious every day. I don't know, Wes. I've never felt like this before, and I've certainly never met someone like her before. I honestly thought that we could keep things strictly professional, but that went out the window after a few weeks." Pelham shook his head. "I can't see a future without her, and frankly, I'm terrified."

"Why?"

"Because we work together. You know as well as anyone how complicated that can be."

"You mean Jeanie?"

Pelham nodded.

Jeanie was Wes' wife, and they had met while working together at the same Madison Avenue agency where Pelham had worked. When they got married, Jeanie left the business so she and Wes wouldn't be caught in the same situation that Pelham now faced. "I guess the big complication is that Natalie is just beginning her career, and you don't want anything to risk that," Wes said. "Jeanie was fine walking away from the advertising game, but I can see that it's different for Natalie."

Pelham agreed. "I don't want her career jeopardized, and I don't want my career jeopardized."

"You remember that I told you there was a solution to that problem, right?" Wes asked.

"You mentioned some options, as I recall," Pelham answered, "but no specifics."

"Well, that's what I'm here to discuss now, since it looks like we'll need to put one of those options into effect."

"What do you have in mind?" Pelham asked.

"You remember Gordon Marteney, don't you?"

Pelham nodded.

Wes outlined a new service Gordon had been working on where the firm would take over the Brand Management functions of a client until the branding could be redesigned, new staff hired and trained, and a mechanism put in place for the firm to monitor the client even after the outsourcing contract was over.

Pelham listened closely, thought about what Wes had presented, and then began asking questions.

"I knew you'd see the flaws in my thinking," Wes said after several minutes. "That's why I like running new ideas past you first. You help me take my crazy ideas and figure out how to implement it in our firm."

They discussed options for nearly an hour before agreeing on a workable solution. "So, you see a place for Natalie working in the new service area?" Pelham asked after he was pleased with the agreements he and Wes had reached.

"Absolutely," Wes replied. "Tell me, who are you planning to have Natalie shadow for the next few months?"

"Nadine Richardson first, and then Briana Knowles."

Love Lost, Love Found

"Nadine is your top publicist, right."

"That's right."

"And Briana is one of your top Brand Managers."

"Also right."

"Would you mind putting Natalie with Briana first? The reason I ask is I want Natalie up to speed on our current Brand Management services. By the time she's proficient with what we do, we'll be ready to start rolling out the new service in your region. We can slide Natalie into one of the open slots, and she'll be part of the new team from the very start. And if Brand Management isn't her thing, we can move her into Publicity services with Nadine. How does that sound?"

"It sounds like a workable solution," Pelham acknowledged.

"Good. Natalie will be working here, she'll be reporting to Gordon, and the two of you can continue carrying on with no conflicts of interest."

"So, Gordon will be in charge of the new service?"

Wes nodded. "He's now the Director of Brand Management Services, and it'll be his show, like training is your show."

"Are you going to run this new service past everyone at the next Partner's meeting?"

"It's first on the agenda," Wes confirmed. "Will I have your support?"

"Of course," Pelham assured him.

After leaving Pelham's office, Wes walked down to Natalie's office and introduced himself. Natalie was still getting her office arranged the way she liked it and adding a few personal touches.

Wes took one look at Natalie in her new blouse, skirt, heels, and her updo hairstyle, and he immediately understood why Pelham found her irresistible.

They chatted for a while, and then Wes made the rounds before he returned to Pelham's office to discuss adding more training staff so he wouldn't have to do all the training by himself.

Beverly Houston arrived right before noon and took Natalie to lunch, so they could get better acquainted. She outlined how the Internship program worked, but she didn't say anything about the new service offering. Then they talked about the firm, the program, and the opportunities that the firm could offer, returning to the office two hours later.

Wes drove Beverly to the airport, so she could catch her flight to Los Angeles for meetings with the interns out there, and then he headed back to Pittsburgh.

For the next two months, Natalie worked with Briana, learning the ins and outs of Brand Management. Natalie accompanied Briana on client visits and helped with research and delivering presentations to existing and prospective clients. She loved the work, and Briana's status reports indicated that Natalie was a natural at working with clients to solve branding issues.

Pelham kept Wes informed about Natalie's skills and interest in branding, and Wes was clearly happy that his plans for Natalie appeared to be on track.

Pelham and Natalie continued growing closer. They spent every weekend together, and at least two to three nights during the week. But Natalie always went home each morning before work, so she could shower and change. Their love grew daily, but they were diligent keeping any evidence of it out of the office.

But something unexpected began to happen. Natalie still had the occasional nightmares—they had lessened once she left Australia, but they had not completely gone away—but they

Love Lost, Love Found

started getting worse. At least once a week, Pelham was awakened by Natalie screaming. He'd have to hold her for quite a while until she was calm enough to go back to sleep.

After a month of this, Pelham suggested that she see somebody to help her get over her nightmares and put Amir behind her once and for all. She agreed.

On a Tuesday in mid-August, Natalie arrived at the office of Dr. Patricia Ramsey, a psychologist who had experience dealing with traumatic relationships.

Natalie explained about the nightmares and about her relationship with Amir. She explained the emotional abuse and the patterns of behavior that kept her from realizing what had been happening to her. She also mentioned her relationship with Pelham, and how different and better it was than the one with Amir.

"What you're experiencing is normal," Dr. Ramsey said. "For four years you were practically living in a reality television show, not being able to distinguish between what was real and what was a prank, and having to deal with everything being recorded. I can't imagine what it was like never knowing if you could believe what was happening around you, and it's no wonder you're suffering from the aftermath of that emotional trauma. The sad part is: it's affecting your current relationship. Deep down, you know that you're in a much better place now, but there's a part of you that still wonders when it will all come crashing down and the cycles that defined your life will start happening again. You're expecting bad things to happen, and that's what's triggering your nightmares. Your conscious mind and your unconscious mind need to be more in sync, so you can move past the trauma and trust your current relationship."

"How do I do that?" Natalie asked.

Dr. Ramsey gave her several suggestions to help confront her fears, and Natalie promised to put them into practice.

For the next two months, Natalie saw Dr. Ramsey once a

week, and in time, the nightmares began to subside.

In early-October, Natalie's parents and brother flew to Maryland for a visit. Pelham let them stay at his house while they were in town.

Natalie's family, and especially her father, was delighted to see how happy Natalie was and how good she looked. She had the poise and confidence of a successful businesswoman, and this helped convince them that moving to the States was the right thing for her.

They stayed for a week, and Pelham showed them around the area and introduced them to Maryland crab, which they all ended up loving. Pelham was also able to have a private conversation with Natalie's father. There was a question that needed to be asked.

After her family left, Natalie seemed sad, and she began interacting more with her friends in Australia via instant messaging and social media.

The afternoon after Natalie's parents flew back to Australia, Pelham contacted Bob Prescott, his attorney.

"What can I do for you, Pelham?" Bob asked.

"I need you to contact the State Department and get some information for me."

"What kind of information?"

Pelham explained what he needed to know. Bob snickered. "Really? Okay, I'll find out for you. I'll call you back once I know what needs to be done."

"Thanks, Bob."

A week after her parents returned to Australia, Natalie and Pelham sat on the soft in the living room, snuggling as they watched television.

Natalie noticed that Pelham wasn't paying attention to the show. He wasn't laughing at the funny parts. "You seem distracted. What's up?"

Pelham looked at her. "I'm not."

"Yes, you are. Out with it. What's going on?"

Pelham looked nervous. "I had something planned for this evening, but I'm trying to decide if it's the right time. That's all."

Natalie looked curious. "What did you have planned?"

Pelham shook his head.

"Pelham, what did you have planned?" Natalie's voice grew more insistent.

"I was going to give you something."

"What?"

Pelham didn't answer.

Natalie's voice grew higher and louder. "Pelham, what were you going to give me?"

Pelham reached into his pocket and took out the ring box. "This," he said as he opened the box.

Inside, set on a yellow-gold band, was a beautiful diamond in the classic round brilliant-cut style that Natalie loved.

"Actually?" Natalie began trembling. "Is that what I think it is?"

Pelham smiled mischievously. "What do you think it is?"

Natalie slid closer to him. "If that's what I think it is, does this mean that you're asking me to marry you? Are you?"

Pelham looked into her eyes. "Yes, I want you to marry me. I want us to be married, to be a family, if that's what you want, too. I don't want to wait any longer to tell you how completely I love you and how I can't stand the thought of living a single day without you."

He took the ring out of the box and slid it onto her finger. "Natalie Patterson, will you be my wife?"

"Too right!" Natalie threw her arms around him. "Yes, I'll marry you and be your wife."

They kissed, and it was electric.

"Wait," Natalie said, looking panicked. "Can I get married in the U.S. with my visa?"

"Bob is looking into it, but the procedure should be fairly simple," Pelham replied.

Natalie kissed him again.

After a while, Natalie pulled back and stared at the ring. Then she said, "How am I supposed to wear this at work? I can't hide it, and once it's seen, everyone will be asking me about it."

Pelham smiled. "I thought about that." He moved a couple of books on the coffee table and extracted another box from its hiding place. This box was longer, wider, and thicker. He handed it to Natalie.

She opened the box, and inside was a beautiful gold chain. "Wear it around your neck on this when you're at the office," Pelham said. "If anyone asks, say it's an heirloom that you got from your family when they were here."

Natalie smiled and hugged Pelham again. "It's lovely, thanks, and that's a great idea. Hiding in plain sight." Natalie got an excited look in her face. "We need to tell my family."

"No," Pelham said. "We only need to tell them that you said yes. They already know I was going to propose."

"What? What?" she asked. "Actually?"

"I talked to your father when your family was here," Pelham explained. "You didn't think I'd propose to you without his blessing, did you?"

Tears were running down Natalie's face, but she was smiling with joy. "You truly are the perfect man for me." She hugged him tightly.

A little while later, after she had dried her eyes, they had a

Love Lost, Love Found

video call with her family to share the good news.

"So, when's the wedding?" Natalie's mother asked.

"We're working on that," Natalie said. "I'll let you know as soon as we figure it out."

"Congratulations," Natalie's father said. "We can't wait to see you two again."

"It won't be long, Dad," Natalie said. "I promise."

As happy as Natalie was about the engagement, she hesitated telling her friends back in Australia, and as it turned out, that was a good thing because not all of Natalie's friends were true friends. One was keeping Amir informed about everything Natalie was doing.

The text message from Amir arrived on the Friday night before Halloween, as Natalie and Pelham were watching television at his house.

Natalie checked her phone, and the blood drained from her face. "What the hell? What the bloody hell?"

"What is it?" Pelham asked.

"I just got a bloody text message from Amir!"

"I didn't think he had your new number."

"He didn't. Someone gave it to him." Natalie looked up at Pelham. "Someone betrayed me and shared my number with him. Now I can't trust any of my old friends in Australia, and I'm going to have to change my phone number… again!"

"What does his text say?" Pelham asked.

Natalie stared at him, and then she looked at her phone. *"Dear Natalie, my love, you've been gone for nearly five months, and by now you surely have finished sowing your wild oats and are realizing how good I was for you—how good we were together. It's time for you to come back to me, and I promise that things will be different. I want to make you a true partner in my life and in business. I've decided to incorporate the video channel in both our names. We'll share in the monetization, and there will be stipulations that, while you and I will prank our friends and family, we will never again prank each other. It'll be like the old days, only it will be a business venture. We'll run it together as true partners.*

"You ripped my heart out, Natalie, but I forgive you. Come home. We'll pick up where we left off, and things will be great. You'll see. I've grown in the time you've been gone. I think you'll like the new me, and I'm sure I'll like the new you. Come home, and we'll do all the things you wanted: live together, get married, start a family, travel. We are soulmates, Natalie, and it's time for you to come back to me. Love Forever, Amir."

Natalie looked up at Pelham, her eyes blazing with fury. "Can you believe that prick bastard? He thinks that I'll forgive him? He thinks that anything he offers me could ever compare with what you and I have? What a lunatic!"

Natalie typed something into her phone and then put it down. She looked at Pelham, still obviously angry.

"What did you say to him?"

"One word: 'No.' Oh, I know he won't accept it, but at least he knows I won't play his game."

"You know he'll escalate now," Pelham pointed out.

Natalie nodded. "I know. He's so predictable. But I've been thinking about what I'll do if he does something online. Dr. Ramsey has been helping me with it."

"What?" Pelham asked.

Natalie explained her plan, and Pelham laughed. "That's brilliant! What a masterstroke! It's sheer genius."

Natalie blushed. "Thank you. I'll need your help to set it up, and we can file that paperwork that your attorney prepared at the same time. He'll see part of what I'm doing, but he'll never see the legal part coming."

Pelham shook his head in amazement. "I am so impressed

Love Lost, Love Found

with you, Natalie. To come up with a plan like this and know exactly how you want to execute it is amazing. I'm... I'm in awe of you right now."

Natalie smiled. Then she cocked her head to one side and asked, "Do you think it will work?"

"I don't know, but it should. Either way, it will shock him to his core, and that might be enough to make him go away forever."

Natalie enjoyed her first American autumn. Then, when the winter snows started falling early, Natalie experienced her first true winter weather. She loved playing in the snow, learning to ski and snowboard, and enjoying some of the other winter sports that the area had to offer.

Natalie had her cell phone number changed, and she had the store install an app to block all of Amir's numbers. She also blocked most of her old friends on social media and dropped them from her phone's contact list. She didn't know who had betrayed her to Amir, and she wasn't going to take any chances that one of them might do it again.

In early December, Pelham scheduled training sessions in Richmond, Charlotte, and Charleston. Natalie went with him to help out, as did the two employees that Pelham had hired to take over the training service. Pelham allowed Natalie to run the workshops and show the new employees how it was done, with Pelham there to advise and evaluate.

They returned to Maryland just before Christmas, and Natalie helped Pelham decorate for the holidays. The weekend before Christmas, Pelham had his annual Christmas party for the office staff and their families. It was a beautiful affair, and everyone had a great time.

Natalie spent the night on Christmas Eve. Although she and

Pelham had agreed that they wouldn't exchange gifts, since they didn't want a long engagement and wanted to keep their money for the wedding and the honeymoon, they each put a few small gifts under the tree for each other.

They made love on Christmas morning, before the sun came up, and afterwards they lay in bed, simply enjoying being close to each other. When they finally got out of bed, Natalie saw that snow had fallen overnight. They both showered together, dressed, and went downstairs to make breakfast. Pelham lit the fireplaces, which all used gas logs, while Natalie made coffee. The firelight, along with the lights from the trees and garlands around the house, gave the house a warm glow that made Natalie finally understand the magic of the Christmas season in wintertime.

"It's sunny and hot at my parent's home right now," Natalie said as they ate breakfast. "If I were there, I'd be barefoot, wearing short shorts and a singlet right now, and we'd probably go swimming this afternoon. Or we'd be on the coast at the beach. Who could have known that a white Christmas was so beautiful?"

After they had opened their gifts, Pelham and Natalie curled up next to each other on the couch. Pelham reached under one of the pillows and pulled out a folder.

"What's this?" Natalie asked.

"All of the forms that have to be filled out to get married under your current visa," Pelham replied.

Natalie opened the folder and found that most of the forms had already been completed. Only a few additional pieces of information were needed, along with Natalie's signatures. In addition, there were a couple of forms and letters that Pelham had to complete, and those were also in the folder.

"Bob did all of this?" Natalie asked, reviewing the papers.

"He did most of the work, but I helped," Pelham confirmed.

"How long will it take for the applications to get

approved?"

"Not too long, but we should get this filed as soon as possible."

Natalie finished looking at the forms and then put the folder on the coffee table. She snuggled close to Pelham. "Thank you. Now that we know this can be done, we should start planning."

"I agree, Pelham said. "What kind of wedding do you want?"

"Small and simple," Natalie said. "If we have it in Maryland, I want my family there, and maybe our co-workers, but no one else, actually."

"Do you want it Maryland or in Australia?"

Natalie thought about it. "Here, I think. Fewer potential problems that way. And since I only want Mom, Dad, Ed, and Aunt Rachel there, it'll be easier to bring them up here than to get everyone else down there."

"May I make a suggestion?" Pelham asked.

"Please do. It's your wedding, too, after all."

Pelham shared an idea he has been thinking about for several weeks. Natalie's face lit up as he described the simple surprise wedding he had in mind.

"I love that," Natalie said. "I especially love the surprise part."

"It'll blow their minds," Pelham said. "Your family will need to know, as will one other person and any of my family who can make it, but no one else."

"Who will be your best man?" Natalie asked.

"Wes," Pelham replied. "He's the only choice. What about your maid of honor?"

"That's tough," Natalie said. "The people we work with are almost the only people I know here in the states."

"What about Rachel?" Pelham suggested.

Natalie grinned. "That's a great suggestion. She's been more of a sister to me anyway, so that's perfect."

"Okay, we have the place worked out and the guest list. All we need to do is set the date."

Natalie stared at the flames crackling in the fireplace. "When is my internship over?"

"Well, you started a bit late, but the program runs from the first of June to the end of May. Why?"

"What do you think about the end of May, when the lease on my corporate apartment runs out. There's a holiday around then, isn't there?"

"Memorial Day," Pelham said.

"Right. What if you invited everyone to a garden party on that Saturday?"

"What kind of attire? Garden parties are usually dressy."

"Dressy is fine," Natalie said. "What do you want us to wear?"

"Nothing too fancy, don't you think?"

Natalie nodded. "I want a simple off-white dress that's easy to move in and doesn't have all that lace and train stuff."

"Do you want it full length or shorter?"

"What are your thoughts?" Natalie asked.

"It'll be hot on Memorial Day, so if you don't mind being non-traditional, shorter might be better."

Natalie nodded. "You'll help me pick it out?"

"If that's what you want, then of course. What would you like me to wear?" he asked.

"What about that kilt I saw in your closet?" Natalie suggested.

Pelham laughed. "You want me dressed in my Scotsman best?"

"Why not? I love your legs, and there's something about a man in a kilt, worn properly, of course."

"Of course. Okay, my kilt it is."

They sat quietly for a while.

"So, is that it?" Natalie asked. "Did we just plan our

wedding?"

Pelham nodded. "All we need now is to plan the honeymoon."

"I like beaches," Natalie said.

"I was thinking Scotland and Ireland," Pelham suggested.

"Can we do both?" Natalie asked.

Pelham looked at her and smiled. "For you, anything."

Chapter 11

As expected, Amir escalated. He posted a video to his channel just after the New Year, and when Natalie saw it, she was livid. She walked into Pelham's office at the house to let him watch it.

"Hi, everyone. It's Amir. Well, if you've been following the saga of 'what happened to Natalie,'—and judging from the comments and messages you've been sending, you have—you probably know that she's living in the United States in the mid-Atlantic coast region. She has confided to her friends here in Australia that she knows now she made a huge mistake leaving me, but she feels trapped by this bloke she has been seeing over there. Clearly, she needs my help to get away from him and return home where she belongs. Her family has even reached out to me, asking for my help. Well, I'm keen to help. I'm making arrangements to fly to the United States, rescue her, and bring her home to her family and me. It's going to take a lot of money to do this, so if any of you are feeling generous and want to contribute to the cause, here's how."

Amir gave information about how fans could send him money to help with the "Natalie Rescue Travel Fund."

"Natalie still has her last video posted to her social media

Love Lost, Love Found

accounts, which obviously means that it wasn't her idea to post it in the first place. That bloke who's trapping her probably made her do it. He and I are going to have words when I get there. If I can record it, I will and then post it so you can see what Natalie has been going through for so long. She needs our help, and she needs our understanding as she gets over all that has happened since she moved to Sydney. More on this as the plans are finalized. God bless."

"Can you believe that jerk?" Natalie shouted in anger once the video ended.

"We knew he was going to escalate, but who knew he'd go so far as to solicit funds so he could fly over here?"

Natalie fumed.

"What does this do to your plan?" Pelham asked.

"Oh, it's on," Natalie stated resolutely. "I need you to have your lawyer file the paperwork he drafted. I'll take care of getting Amir to agree to the live stream we discussed."

"We should probably notify the State Department so Amir can be placed on the No-Fly list, and petitioning for a restraining order to keep him away from you if he should come here is also a good idea."

Natalie nodded. "Can your lawyer take care of that, too?"

"I'll find out." Pelham looked up the video online and sent the link via email to Bob Prescott, asking him to look into the No-Fly List and the restraining order.

"What now?" Pelham asked.

"I call Amir and put the other part of the plan into motion."

"Why don't you call from the house line? The caller id is blocked, so he won't have this number. Plus, I can have his number blocked, just in case."

"Okay," Natalie agreed.

Amir heard his phone ring. Looking at the caller id, all he could tell was that the call originated from the United States. He smiled. *That didn't take long. I knew Natalie would be calling when she saw the latest video.*

"Hello, Natalie," he said smugly, trying not to sound triumphant. "To what do I owe the pleasure of this call?"

"Amir," Natalie acknowledged with little emotion. "I think you know the reason."

"Ah, calling to admit defeat? Do you want me to fly over and help you pack, or are you going to leave everything behind when you come back to me?"

"I'm calling to ask you nicely—one last time—to stop this and leave me alone. If you don't, I won't be responsible for what happens next."

"There's nothing you can do to me, Natalie, but obviously there's still lots I can do to you. I warned you not to mess with me, and if you don't come home right now, you'll understand why."

"There's no need for threats," Natalie said smoothly. "What about a compromise… one that the fans should absolutely love."

"I'm listening." Amir sounded intrigued.

"You set up a live streaming session on your video channel. Just you and me. Live. Unedited. Unrehearsed. Promote it on your channel and social media accounts, so all of the fans have a chance to tune in and watch."

"What would the purpose be?" Amir asked.

"For you to state your case to me why I should come back to you," Natalie said. "You'll go first and make your case for why I should ever trust you again, and then I'll go last and state why I don't think it's in my best interest. I have to let you speak uninterrupted, and you have to let me speak uninterrupted. No editing, no lost connections, nothing but us getting to speak our minds."

"And why would I agree to that, Natalie?" Amir demanded.

Love Lost, Love Found

"Because if you make a good enough case, I'll be on the next flight home," Natalie replied. "And if I make a good enough case, you'll leave me alone. And if we can't agree, then we'll hire an impartial professional arbitrator who will review our cases and make the decision for us—binding on us both."

"That doesn't sound like a good idea to me, Natalie."

"What are you afraid of, Amir? Worried you can't make a case that any rational person would think was good enough? Scared of what I might say?"

Natalie knew that comment would infuriate Amir.

"Why should I be afraid of anything you might say?" he demanded. "I can certainly make a case that our fans will support and that some arbitrator would find compelling."

"Then what are you afraid of?"

"I'm not afraid," Amir roared. "All right. Fine. A live stream between the two of us. When do you want to do this?"

"How about next weekend? Remember, there's a fourteen-hour difference between here and there, so make it a time when we're both awake, okay?"

"Okay." Amir sounded triumphant. "You're such a fool, Natalie. You've never won an argument with me. You're in way over your head this time."

"We'll see, Amir. We'll see. Send me the links to the live stream via email once you have it set up. Oh, and you have to promise to leave the recording of the live stream on your channel for at least a week. Okay?"

Amir snorted. "I promise. What's your new email address?"

Natalie gave Amir an email address she had just set up online. It would be used for the live stream only, and then it would be deleted.

"And Amir…" Natalie began.

"What?"

"No tricks. Don't try to keep me from getting into the live stream so you can make it look like I chickened out. Got it?"

"Go it, Natalie. No tricks."

Natalie ended the call.

Pelham and Natalie looked at each other and started laughing. "He fell for it," Pelham said.

"I knew he would," Natalie stated. "Once he gets angry, he stops thinking clearly. It's his biggest weakness."

"Are you ready to go through with it?"

Natalie nodded. "Can you disguise my IP address when I log into the live stream?"

"Sure," Pelham replied. "The WiFi here in the house is on a secure VPN. No IP addresses are visible."

Natalie looked pleased. "So, if we can get all the paperwork filed before Saturday, I can hit him with the Cease-and-Desist letters, the court petition to take down all my content, the No-Fly list, and the restraining order all at the same time. If that doesn't shake him to the core, nothing will."

"Are you going to tell him that you're engaged?"

Natalie beamed. "Of course. I'm going to throw in his face that you did something after less than a year that he wouldn't do in four years. It'll show everyone just how little he actually cared about me."

"You know Wes will be watching that live stream?"

"You haven't told him yet?" Natalie sounded surprised. "I guess you should."

Pelham nodded and dialed Wes' number.

Wes answered the phone. "Pelham, it's the weekend! I love your dedication, but take some time off, buddy."

"This won't take long," Pelham said. "There's been a development on the Amir front."

"What's happening?"

Pelham brought Wes up to speed on what Amir had done and what Natalie's solution to the problem was. Pelham also let Wes know about what his lawyer was working on.

"That's terrific!" Wes said. "Well done. I can't wait to

Love Lost, Love Found

watch the live stream. Be sure to send me the link."

"I will, but that brings up another point that I need to mention. You'll hear something on the live stream that you need to hear from me first. I don't want you blindsided."

"What's that?"

"Natalie and I are getting married," Pelham said.

There was silence on the call. Then Pelham heard Wes shout, "Jeanie! Come here, quick!"

A moment later, Pelham heard Jeanie's voice. "What's up?"

"Say that again, Pelham," Wes said.

"I said that Natalie and I are getting married."

Jeanie squealed, and Wes laughed. "That's great news! When's the big day?"

Pelham told Wes and Jeanie about the surprise wedding they had planned and how no one apart from Natalie's family knew about it. "I need to make sure that both of you will be there," Pelham said after revealing the plans.

"Of course, we'll be there," Jeanie stated.

"Why do you need to make sure of that?" Wes asked.

"Because I want you to be my best man," Pelham said.

"I'm... I'm honored, Pelham," Wes said. "I'd be thrilled to be your best man. We wouldn't miss this wedding for the world."

"Thanks, Wes."

"Any time, my friend. Good luck to the both of you, and congratulations! Oh, and great job with Amir. I'll be watching the live stream with popcorn. Let's talk next week."

Pelham agreed and ended the call. He looked at Natalie, who was smiling. "That went well."

"I need to ask Aunt Rachel to be my maid of honor," Natalie said.

"Why not call her now?" Pelham asked.

Natalie nodded. She placed the call to Rachel, who answered it on the second ring. As expected, Rachel agreed immediately. After chatting for a while, Natalie ended the call.

"That's done," Natalie said.

"Why didn't you tell her about Amir?"

"I'm going to tell my entire family by email as soon as I get the link from Amir."

Pelham stood. "Well, after all that, I'm hungry. What do you want for dinner?"

Pelham talked to Bob Prescott first thing Monday morning.

"That was some video," Bob said.

"Yes, it was," Pelham agreed. "And the conversation with Amir that followed was something, too."

"You two talked to Amir?"

Pelham filled Bob in about the live stream coming up on Saturday.

"That's risky, Pelham," Bob said. "Very risky."

"Yes, but it's bold, and it just might shake him off his feet, so he'll leave her alone. And if we can hit him with what I've asked you to do on the live stream, it'll show him that he lost and should surrender before he finds himself getting arrested."

"Speaking of that, I already contacted the District Attorney's office about the restraining order, and after watching the video, they see no problem getting a judge to sign off on it. I also have a call with the State Department this afternoon. Incidentally, I'll be requesting that Amir be on both the No-Fly List and the Travel Ban, so he can't enter the country legally by any means: land, sea, or air."

"Great thinking, Bob," Pelham said. "Keep me posted."

"Will do. Oh, and send me a link to the live stream. I want to watch it."

"I will." Pelham ended the call.

Amir sent the live stream links—the link to watch the live stream and the participant link for Natalie alone to use—and Natalie forwarded the link to watch the live stream to Pelham, Dr. Ramsey, and her family. Pelham forwarded the link to Wes and Bob.

The live stream was scheduled for Saturday night, which would be mid-morning Sunday in Brisbane.

By the time Saturday arrived, Natalie seemed calm and resolute. Pelham was a ball of nervous energy. He helped Natalie set up her laptop on his desk. He'd be in the office with her, but he'd be watching the live stream with his headphones on from his side of the desk, while Natalie participated in the live steam from the other side of the desk.

Bob got back to Pelham on Friday with the restraining order and confirmation that Amir had been added to the No-Fly List and the Travel Ban list, which was being distributed to all points of entry across the United States. He also reported that the video channel hosting company had been served with the Cease-and-Desist letters and the court petitions for all content that contained Natalie to be removed from Amir's channel. Everything was ready for the live stream.

Ten minutes before the live stream was to begin, Natalie logged into the site so she could set up her audio and video. Pelham sat across from her, ready to watch the spectacle and to root for the love of his life.

At nine o'clock, Eastern Time, the live stream started.

"Hello everyone," Amir said smugly. "This is Amir."

"And this is Natalie," she said.

"And this is our first live stream," Amir continued. "In case you didn't see the announcement, I'm in Brisbane and Natalie is in America. I've asked her to come back to Australia, and she is hesitant. But she has agreed to let me state my case, live in front of all of you, and if she thinks I've made my case, she promises to be on the next plane home. But she also gets to state her case for remaining in America, and if I think she has made her case, then I have to leave her alone forever. But if we can't agree, she has agreed to binding arbitration to settle the issue once and for all. Does that sound right, Natalie?"

"That's what we agreed to, Amir."

"And you still want me to go first?" he asked.

"Of course," Natalie said.

Amir began his presentation about why Natalie should come back to him. He didn't acknowledge his actions to track her every movement, nor did he repeat his accusations that she was part of a cult or with someone who was keeping her trapped. Instead, he talked about the good times, all that he had done for her, all that he had given her, the trips they took, the money that the video channel generated, and his plans for the future, including the business partnership, getting married, and starting a family. He ended by reminding her that they were soulmates and that they were destined to be together forever.

Amir had a triumphant look on his face when he finished. "How was that, Natalie?"

"Old news, Amir. Old news." Natalie yawned. "Some of it was even true. Much of it wasn't, or was only true from your perspective. But, it's my turn, and I'm not going to comment further about what you said. I'm going to state my case for staying in America and you leaving me alone forever."

Natalie saw Amir's confident expression slip as an angry sneer flashed across his face before he regained control. She just smiled and began telling her side of the story.

"I have a hard time believing that it's necessary to emotionally abuse and traumatize a soulmate, to stalk and electronically track a soulmate, or to bribe a soulmate to stay with you, but that's what you did from the time we met until the time I moved to the United States, Amir."

Love Lost, Love Found

 Natalie proceeded to call out every hurtful, terrible thing that Amir had ever done, from the first time he pranked her until he caused her to miss her Consulate interview. She detailed the emotional abuse of four years and the cycle of behavior that is so typical in an abusive relationship, even when physical abuse has yet to be manifested.

 "I told you what I thought of you after you got back from Seoul," she said, recapping her conversation with Amir before she left for Sydney. "I told you it was over, I told you I no longer loved you, and I told you to never contact me again. Did you do as I asked? No, you followed me to Sydney, terrorizing me by stalking me and tracking my whereabouts with GPS tags that you secreted in all my things, including my purse, my phone, and my car. Did you think that terrorizing me would make me love you again? Or was that just an indication of what a future with you in it would be like? Doesn't sound like soulmates to me. It sounds like obsession, and to a woman, an obsession like yours is dangerous, not loving. You're unstable, Amir. You've proven it by mobilizing your fans to hunt me down and tell you where I am, by telling your fans that I'm being held against my will, by convincing my so-called friends to betray me by giving you my new phone numbers, and by threatening to come to America to 'rescue' me when the only person I need rescuing from is you.

 "What I finally realized, after getting away from you, is that you only love one thing: the attention you get from your video channel. I'm a means to an end, and while I believe that you're sincere about forming a partnership to manage the channel, you never said that it'll be an equal partnership, and I don't believe for a moment that you'd ever let me be an equal. You'll keep the lion's share for yourself, controlling me with the promise of more, but that's a promise you'll never keep, just like your promise to love me, to marry me, to start a family with me, and to stop emotionally traumatizing me.

 "Realizing all that, and knowing that you're incapable of

changing, here are some additional reasons why I'm remaining in the United States."

Natalie held up her left hand. "First of all, I'm engaged to be married. That's right Amir, the one thing you couldn't commit to in over four years, I've found someone who—in less than one year—already knows he wants to spend the rest of his life with me. And he has never traumatized me, electronically tracked me, stalked me, embarrassed me in front of my friends and family, lied to me, or used me to entertain others. He treats me with respect, he wants only what's best for me, even at the risk of his own career, and he'll do anything for me. He is the best man I've ever met. He even asked for my father's blessing before proposing. He's the man I'm going to spend the rest of my life with, Amir. Not you."

Natalie held up a stack of papers. "Second, this is a restraining order. It's a court order that says you cannot come within five hundred yards of me, which is four hundred and fifty seven meters for those of you in Australia. If you violate this court order, you'll go to jail in America."

Natalie showed the next document. "This is a notice from the United States Department of State, confirming that you have been placed on a No-Fly List and a Travel Ban list, meaning that you cannot legally enter the United States. Ever. By the way, you might want to refund the money your fans donated to cover your travel expenses, now that it's impossible for you to travel here."

Natalie showed the next document. "This is a Cease-and-Desist letter that is being sent to you and to the hosting company of your video channel. It turns out that you cannot use my likeness in a photograph or video for a commercial purpose without my written permissions, and that means my permission for every instance, not one permission for all content. It's illegal for you to make money off of my likeness without paying me, and you never shared the proceeds of the channel's monetization. So, this letter demands that all content containing my likeness be

Love Lost, Love Found

taken down permanently from your channel. And, since you use your social media merely as advertising for the channel, your social media posts are... as spelled out in the letter... furtherance of the illegal use of my likeness, and all content across all of your social media platforms must be removed as well."

Natalie held up the next document. "This is a court petition filed this week seeking a court order to force the hosting company of your channel to remove all content containing my likeness, and then to deactivate your channel altogether for repeated and... flagrant... violations of United States law."

Natalie put the papers down. "I'm done playing games with you, Amir. I'm done being nice about what you've done and what you're trying to still do to me. If you want war, I'll show you what real war is. You may be bigger, meaner, and tougher than I am physically, which you used to your advantage to keep me in line for years, Amir, but when you're not around to intimidate me physically, then you'll get to see just how strong I am, how resolute I am, and how willing I am to fight fire with fire. You want to control me for the rest of my life. Well, here's my response: Scorched Earth. You robbed me of my joy, you treated me like dirt, and you have proven repeatedly that you're a liar who cannot be trusted. Well, I'm getting back at you in the way that hurts you the most, like you found the ways to hurt me the most. I'm going after what you love most in this world: that stupid video channel. No more pranks, no more fans, no more money, and no more me. Still want me back now?"

Natalie stared at Amir, watching his face go from triumph to shock, to panic, to rage. His face was bright red, and he was gasping, trying to find the words to express his anger.

"Nothing to say to that, Amir? Didn't think I had it in me? Thought you were untouchable? That there's nothing I could do to you as bad as what you did to me for *four years*? My biggest mistake was showing you all the ways I was vulnerable. It showed you how to abuse me, control me, hurt me. But your mistake was letting me see the one place where *you* were vulnerable, and I unleashed my fury on that one thing, and I'll watch it burn to the ground to prove to you that I don't love you, I'll never love you, and I'll never come back to you. Do you understand now, Amir, what I'm willing to do to be free of you? So, again I ask, do you still want me back now?"

Amir continued to sputter, and then he shouted, "You Bloody Bitch! I effing hate you! How dare you? How could you do this to me? I never want to see you again as long as I live, you heartless, ungrateful little whore! I'm done with you. It's over. I hope you die!"

Natalie smiled at the camera. "And there you have it, fans. Amir made his case, and it failed to sway me. I made my case, and it convinced Amir to let me go and leave me alone forever. You all heard it. Back it up and listen again if you missed it, but do it quickly, because I'm sure that Amir will either take this down immediately, or the hosting company will when they delete his channel. By the way, my fiancé captured the entire video, so if Amir takes it down, I can post it somewhere else for all of you to see."

Natalie's smile never faded as Amir continued shouting a steady stream of profanities and insults at her for what she had done. After a moment, Natalie waved to the camera. "Bye!"

She signed off of the live stream, took off her headphones, and leaned back in her chair.

"Tell me you captured all of that," she implored.

Pelham checked the recording. It was all there. "I got it." He made a backup of the recording. Then he stood up and walked around the desk, kneeling next to her, he hugged her tightly. "I am so proud of you. You were a total bad ass! You smoked him."

Natalie hugged him. "I can't believe that worked. Once I got him mad, I knew I had him. But to watch him lose it like that on his own channel… it was incredible. Now his fans see what I

Love Lost, Love Found

used to see when he got mad."

"I understand the nightmares now," Pelham said softly. "If I hadn't seen him melt down like that, I don't think I would've ever fully understood it—"

Pelham was interrupted by the phone ringing. It was Wes.

"That was outstanding, Natalie," Wes said when Pelham put him on speakerphone.

"Thanks, Wes," Natalie said. "I'm just glad it's over."

"I've never been more impressed by anyone like I am with the way you conducted yourself. You should have been a lawyer, but I'm grateful to have you on our team. I see great things for you in the future."

"You don't know how happy it makes me to hear that," Natalie said.

"Then you'll love to hear this," Wes said. "We're offering you a permanent position with the firm. You don't even have to finish out the internship. There's an opening in our new Brand Management outsourcing service, and it's yours if you want it. You'll still work in Bethesda, along with two others who are transferring down there shortly, and you'll report to Gordon Marteney here in Pittsburgh. That will keep you in a different chain of command from Pelham, so your relationship won't be an issue at all."

Natalie sat straight up in her chair. "Actually?"

"Yes," Wes assured her. "I can give you the details of the job on Monday morning, or Pelham can give them to you tonight, but it's something we've been grooming you for ever since that day I stopped by the office. You're a natural for what we want you to do, and everyone who has worked with you thinks so." Wes then outlined the compensation package.

Natalie was stunned at the offer. She looked at Pelham and mouthed, "Do I want this job?"

Pelham nodded enthusiastically.

"Okay, Wes. I accept the offer. When does it start?"

"Two weeks from now, when the other two you'll be working with arrive."

"And when do I need to be out of the corporate apartment, since that's tied to the internship program?"

Wes laughed. "I'll let you and Pelham work that out between you. Good night and congratulations again for putting that Amir in his place. Great job!"

Wes ended the call.

"What did Wes mean about the corporate apartment?" Natalie asked.

The phone rang again. This time it was Bob.

"Congratulations, Natalie," Bob said.

"Thanks, Bob. And thanks for everything you did to help."

"It was my pleasure. I'll keep you posted on the court filings." Bob ended the call.

Before Natalie could ask Pelham her question again, her laptop notified her that she had a video chat coming in.

Over the next hour, she had video chats with her parents, her brother, and her aunt, and she received a phone call from Dr. Ramsey. Everyone wanted to congratulate her for the way she handled herself and put Amir in his place.

It was nearly eleven when she was finally able to check to make sure that the video was still on Amir's channel. It was. She checked the comments, and they were overwhelmingly supportive of her. She also noticed that the number of subscribers to the channel had dropped considerably.

She shut down her computer and looked at Pelham. "The corporate apartment," she reminded him. "What did Wes mean?"

"It means you can move out anytime between now and when the new job officially starts," Pelham said.

"I have to get a new place that soon? What if I can't find a place nearby?"

"I can think of a perfect place that's very close by. In fact, you won't find a better price in the entire region."

Love Lost, Love Found

Natalie stared at him, too tired to realize what he was talking about.

"Here," Pelham said, gesturing around the house. "Move in here... with me."

Natalie's eyes widened. "Actually?"

"Of course. Why not?"

"But I thought we were trying to keep people from the office from knowing about us."

"They don't. And once you start the new position, you're going to be so busy with your new team that no one will notice you coming and going from the same direction that I do. We'll keep driving to and from work separately, but you'll live here. You already know which side of the closet is yours."

Natalie stood and threw her arms around Pelham. "Thank you! When do you want to do this?"

"Well, tomorrow's Sunday, and I hate moving on Sundays. There's no time to relax afterwards. How about next weekend? We can pack your things this week, move them on Saturday morning, use the afternoon and evening to put everything away, and then have Sunday to relax and recover."

Natalie hugged him tighter. "Yes. Yes, yes, yes!"

She looked at Pelham in the eyes. "I love you, Pelham."

"I love you, too, Natalie."

It should be noted that Amir never bothered or attempted to contact Natalie ever again. His video channel was deleted by the hosting company, and he was permanently banned from ever posting content with Natalie's likeness on any of his social media platforms.

Natalie and Pelham never knew what eventually happened to Amir, and neither did Natalie's family. In time, even Natalie's nightmares went away.

Chapter 12

The move from the corporate apartment to Pelham's house went smoothly, since all they were moving were clothes and a few personal items. Once everything was loaded into Pelham's SUV, they both straightened up the apartment, so it would be ready for the management company's cleaning service.

Natalie was so happy that she sang to herself as she unpacked and put everything away in the master closet.

Months earlier, Pelham had given her a garage door opener, so she could park in the third garage bay when she came over. He had also given her the remotes for the gate and the alarm system, and her own set of keys to the house.

"Should I keep leasing a car, or should I buy one?" Natalie asked once her car was in the garage and her things upstairs.

"It's your choice," Pelham said. "Your living expenses have just dropped considerably, since there's no need for you to pay rent, insurance, or utilities to live here. But you might want to wait until after the wedding to make a decision. You don't want to spend that much money right before the honeymoon!"

Natalie nodded. "That makes sense."

The two people transferring from Pittsburgh, Emmet Franklin and David Vaughan, arrived two weeks after the live stream with Amir. Natalie joined them in the new office space at the far end of the Carriage House. This made room for the two people who were taking over Pelham's training services to sit closer to the rest of the team members who reported to Pelham. This brought the size of the office staff to fifteen, not counting Pelham.

After a few days to allow the transferring staff to get settled, Natalie began learning the ins and outs of the outsourcing business and how it was being adapted for Brand Management. She loved the concept, and she appreciated being part of the team from the beginning.

The team worked closely with Pelham's Brand Management staff and the sales team to identify existing clients who might benefit from outsourcing. Natalie appreciated being included in sales meetings and on sales calls to prospective clients. It didn't take long for the team to sign their first two outsourcing contracts, and Natalie found herself busier than ever before. She was having the time of her life.

Since Pelham and Natalie's birthdays were only a month apart, and Natalie's was in March close to Easter, Pelham took her for a long weekend at Biltmore in Ashville, North Carolina, to celebrate. She was amazed by the house and the grounds, and she loved walking the trails along the hills and ridges surrounding the estate. It was one of the most fun weekends she had ever had.

With the wedding plans completed, all that remained was selecting the caterer, creating the menu, hiring the musician, and sending out the invitations.

Since the wedding was going to be a surprise, the garden party invitations could hardly contain wedding registry information. Natalie and Pelham decided to forgo registering for wedding gifts. After all, Pelham already had everything they could ever need, and all Natalie wanted was Pelham.

Natalie and Pelham went shopping for Natalie's dress in late March. The more she looked, the less she wanted anything similar to a wedding dress. She wanted a cute but modest white or off-white dress that was cut just above the knee. She finally found what she was looking for. It was white lace from the waist up with a halter neck that showed off her beautiful shoulders. From the waist down, it was an A-Line, semi-sheer, woven white fabric. The skirt had a high waist, and the flared hem stopped three inches above the knee. Natalie looked stunning in the dress with the matching pair of shoes she bought. Pelham thought she looked angelic.

Bob left Pelham a voice mail in Late March. "I thought you'd like to know that the State Department approved the paperwork you filed. Natalie will need to file a Change of Status form after the wedding to speed up her Green Card application, but apart from that, everything's all set. I'll get that form to you this week."

The invitations went out in early April, and the office staff all RSVP'd within a couple of days. Wes and Jeanie had already RSVP'd, and Pelham had made arrangements to fly Natalie's family—Charles, Brenda, Ed, and Rachel—from Australia. Three of Pelham's cousins, who still lived in the area, RSVP'd, bringing the total guest list to thirty-eight, not counting Pelham and Natalie. There was also the harpist—Katie Byrne—the officiant, who was a close friend of Pelham's, the photographer, and the six caterers.

Love Lost, Love Found

Once the weather turned warmer, Natalie began swimming every day in the pool and sunbathing every afternoon when she got home from work. She also sunbathed each weekend, wanting to build a base tan before the wedding and the honeymoon.

As Memorial Day weekend approached, plans moved into high gear for the party. Natalie's parents arrived on the Wednesday before the wedding, and they planned to fly back to Australia on Sunday, the same day that Natalie and Pelham would be leaving on their honeymoon.

The caterers began setting up on Friday, since the party was scheduled to begin at ten-thirty the next morning. Natalie could hardly contain her excitement. That afternoon, the officiant arrived, and they had a quick rehearsal with Natalie's family in attendance. Afterward, Pelham grilled dinner for everyone. It was a happy time for all.

The next morning, Pelham and Natalie rose early and showered. Then they went downstairs for a quick breakfast with Natalie's family before returning upstairs to get ready.

"I can't decide if I want my hair up or down," Natalie said, staring at herself in the mirror.

"Can't you do both?" Pelham asked. "I've seen styles that were partially up and partially down. Or you could braid your hair over one shoulder. Honestly, anything you do will look spectacular."

"You're no help," Natalie pouted. "But thanks for the compliment."

She continued staring at her hair in the mirror until an idea came to her. She began styling it at a frenzied pace to be downstairs before ten-thirty, when the guests were expected.

At Natalie's request, Pelham wore a dark vest over a white dress shirt with his kilt. His kilt hose were off-white cable-knit wool, and he wore plain black leather shoes. He also wore a traditional sporran made of black and silver fur with black leather and silver accents.

When he presented himself so she could see his outfit, Natalie insisted that he turn around so she could see all of him.

"Very nice," she said. "Are you wearing it properly?"

Pelham lifted the front of his kilt, so she could see.

She giggled. "Thank you for that. I honestly never thought I'd get flashed on my wedding day."

"What about me?"

Natalie looked at him, smiled, and untied her robe and let it slide off her shoulders. Pelham was mesmerized by her beautiful tanned skin with no tan lines, made possible by the high walls around the house. "You're gorgeous."

"Save it for later," she purred. "Wedding first, reception second, ripping off each other's clothes third."

"Yes, Dear."

As much as Pelham wanted to leave Natalie alone so she could get ready without him seeing the finished product until the ceremony began, the nature of the event meant that she'd have to be downstairs with him when the guests began arriving.

To keep busy, he went into the bedroom and straightened it up so that it would be presentable to anyone wandering through the house. He had just finished making the bed when he heard a sound behind him. He turned.

Natalie was standing there with her dress and shoes on. Her tan made the dress stand out against her smooth skin. Her hair was lovely, and while the style was still an updo, it hung low in the back. Her makeup was minimal, but it accentuated her eyes and lips without looking inappropriate for a morning party. She turned around for him so he could see the whole outfit.

"My God, you look lovely," he said. He noticed that she had not put on any jewelry. "I have a gift for you."

"Pelham, you've given me enough already."

Pelham went to his dresser and pulled out two boxes. The first one contained a pearl necklace, and the other contained matching earrings.

Love Lost, Love Found

"They're beautiful, Pelham, thank you! You shouldn't have, but thank you."

Natalie put them on and admired her wedding jewelry in the mirror. "They're perfect," she said as she fought back the tears.

"No crying today, Natalie," Pelham said.

She nodded. "Where are the rings?"

Pelham reached into the pocket of his vest and pulled out the wedding bands. Natalie was wearing her engagement ring openly—the first time in front of her co-workers.

Pelham put the bands back into his vest pocket. Then he looked at the time. "We need to go downstairs. Wes and Jeanie should be here any minute, and the rest should start arriving shortly."

As they left the bedroom, Pelham whispered, "Are you ready for this, Miss Patterson?"

"I've never been more ready, Mr. Campbell."

Wes and Jeanie arrived just as Natalie and Pelham reached the main floor.

"Don't you two look terrific," Wes said. The photographer, who had arrived thirty minutes earlier, began taking pictures.

Natalie's family joined them a few minutes later. Natalie introduced her family to Wes, who then introduced Jeanie to the Pattersons and Rachel Bennett.

As the guests arrived, the caterers directed everyone to the pool area where they were given beverages and told that there would be an announcement shortly. By ten-forty, all of the guests had arrived.

Pelham, Natalie, Natalie's family, Wes and Jeanie, Pelham's cousins, and the officiant, stepped onto the patio overlooking the pool area. The photographer was in position in the pool area.

"Good morning, my friends," Pelham said. "I'm glad to see you all here today, and I hope you'll forgive the deception that brought you all here."

There was a murmur from the guests.

Pelham continued. "Those of you who have been to my home know that I don't have any gardens, just landscaping that keeps everything green, so it should be apparent to many of you that this isn't actually a garden party. But it is a celebration, and I thank you all for coming to share it with us."

Pelham gestured to Natalie's family. "These fine people are Natalie's family from Australia: her father Charles Patterson, her mother Brenda Patterson, her brother Ed Patterson, and her aunt Rachel Bennett." He then gestured toward Wes and Jeanie. "And you all know Wes Mason and his wife Jeanie, who came down from Pittsburgh to be here today."

Pelham then introduced his cousins and their spouses. Lastly, he introduced the officiant.

"Dr. Malcom Johansson is a good friend of mine and is, among other things, a wedding officiant in the state of Maryland. This is important for today's festivities, since this is actually a wedding."

The guests all gasped, and when Natalie stood next to Pelham and took his hand, they began to cheer.

"Surprise!" Pelham and Natalie said to the guests.

"We didn't want a big, elaborate affair," Pelham added, "so we thought up this idea. We hope you don't mind. We wanted you all at our wedding, which is happening... well, right now."

Pelham's cousins took their place on the right, and Natalie's parents took their place on the left. Wes stood next to Pelham, and Rachel stood next to Natalie.

Dr. Johansson took his place in the center and began the ceremony, which was short by design. Pelham handed him the wedding bands for the blessing, and then Dr. Johansson presented Natalie's band to Pelham and Pelham's band to

Love Lost, Love Found

Natalie, so they could place the rings on each other's fingers.

After the vows had been exchanged, Dr. Johansson said, "What has been joined here today in the sight of God and this company, let no one attempt to tear apart. By the power vested in me by the church and the state of Maryland, I pronounce you husband and wife. You may now kiss."

The crowd cheered as Pelham and Natalie kissed.

Dr. Johansson then said, "I now have the very great honor of presenting Mr. Jamieson Pelham Campbell and Mrs. Natalie Katherine Campbell."

Everyone cheered again.

The party was a happy affair. As soon as the wedding concluded, waiters descended on the crowd carrying champagne and food. Katie, the harpist, was set up on the far end of the front porch. She did an outstanding job, and her music resonated in every corner of the party.

Dr. Johansson left as soon as the service concluded. He had another wedding to officiate that day, and it was a long drive to the venue.

Lauren was the first to come up and congratulate the happy couple. "I can't believe you kept this a secret from me," she said happily. "How long have you two…"

"Since Australia," Pelham admitted, "but we got engaged back around Halloween."

Lauren's shock was evident. "I can't believe I didn't pick up on it."

"Be sure to tell that to Wes," Pelham said. "It was one of the conditions of Natalie working out of our office."

Lauren laughed and headed for the nearest waiter holding a food tray.

Pelham's cousins enjoyed chatting with Natalie and her

family. *No one can resist that accent.*

The wedding cake was brought out at noon, and after Pelham and Natalie cut the first slice, the caterers took over cutting the cake and passing out the slices. It was a lemon poppy cake with butter cream frosting, and it was delicious.

Once the cake was gone, the party began winding down. Wes and Jeanie left so they could drive back to Pittsburgh, and Pelham's cousins left shortly after that. Then the rest of the guests trickled out, followed by the harpist and the photographer, who promised to have the photos ready by the time Natalie and Pelham returned from their honeymoon.

The caterers packed up the few leftovers and the serving pieces, and loaded everything into their vans. Once they left, only Natalie's family remained.

"I don't know about t'e rest of you, but I'm stuffed," Charles said, taking off his jacket and sitting on the living room couch. "I don't t'ink I could eat another bite until Monday."

"Oh, I doubt that, Dad," Natalie said. "I give you an hour. Maybe two. And you'll be looking for something to eat."

"Maybe t'ree," Charles countered.

"Maybe two," Natalie insisted.

"Has she been t'is way since you've known her?" Charles asked Pelham.

"She's someone who knows what she wants and goes after it, if that's what you're asking," Pelham said. "But if you're asking me to get in between a father and his daughter, I say you're on your own."

They sat around and talked for several hours before everyone decided to have a small supper before turning in for the night. The airport shuttle was picking up Natalie's family at five the next morning, and she and Pelham were leaving at ten.

Pelham escorted Natalie upstairs. When he closed the bedroom doors, Natalie removed her pearl necklace and earrings. Then she asked, "How are we going to enjoy our wedding night properly? My parents are downstairs!"

"Don't worry," he said, removing his vest. "There are no bedrooms below this one, and the way this house is built, no sound from this room can escape this room. You have nothing to worry about."

"Are you sure?" she asked as Pelham removed his shirt.

"Completely sure." He came up behind her and unzipped the dress from the neck to just past the curve of her behind. He pulled the back of the dress open, and it slid down to the floor. Then he picked it up and laid it on one of the nearby chairs.

Natalie was wearing a pair of white lace high-cut panties and her shoes. Nothing else. Pelham nuzzled her neck.

Natalie kicked off her shoes as Pelham removed his sporran. He then removed his shoes and the kilt hose.

They turned to face each other. Pelham unbuckled the straps that held his kilt on, and Natalie removed her panties.

"You're absolutely certain?" she asked breathlessly as she looked at Pelham standing in front of her.

"Does it really matter?" Pelham asked as he put his arms around her.

Natalie's family left for the airport the next morning. Natalie and Pelham had just enough time to throw something on and race downstairs to see them off in the airport shuttle.

Once the shuttle left, they went back upstairs to hang up their wedding clothes, shower, and pack for their honeymoon. They were flying to Nassau in the Bahamas that day, staying at The Ocean Club for three nights. Then they were flying to Edinburgh and Inveraray for a few days before heading over to Dublin and Galway, where Natalie's father was born. They had to pack for two distinctly different climates, but they didn't care. They were too excited to be able to spend time together openly.

No more hiding their relationship from anyone.

Their plane landed in Nassau on time, and soon an open-air limo was whisking them down the coast to The Ocean Club. They checked in, changed, and headed for the beach to enjoy the late afternoon sunshine. As soon as they dipped their toes into the warm tropical water, they felt at peace. All of the craziness from the past fourteen months seemed like a distant memory. They walked along the beach, hand in hand.

"What do you want to do first, Mrs. Campbell?" Pelham asked as the sun sank lower toward the horizon.

"Go back to the room and spend the rest of the evening and night in bed, Mr. Campbell."

They raced back to the hotel as fast as they could. When they got there, room service had delivered a large basket filled with fruit, chocolate, champagne, and other delectables. "Keep that close by," Natalie said and she removed her swimsuit. "We're going to need something to keep our strength up."

"Anything you want, my love."

The End

ABOUT THE AUTHOR

Award-winning author and publisher William Speir was born in 1962 in Birmingham, Alabama. He attended the University of Alabama, and graduated from the University of Alabama at Birmingham in 1984. He spent over 25 years in corporate America, serving as a management consultant, leader, IT executive, and HR/Payroll executive for top-tier consulting firms and Fortune 100 companies.

During William's corporate career, he published several articles on leadership and the human impact of organizational changes and technology changes.

His first experience with book publishing was with a series of ten textbooks he authored about field artillery in the 19th century. These textbooks were later consolidated into a single volume and re-published in 2015 as *Muzzle-Loading Artillery for Reenactors*.

In addition to his artillery manual, William has published 21 novels, including a 9-book action-adventure series (*The Knights of the Saltire Series*), five historical novels (*King's Ransom, The Saga of Asbjorn Thorleikson, Nicaea – The Rise of the Imperial Church, Arthur, King,* and *The Besieged Pharaoh*), one fantasy novel (*The Kingstone of Airmid*), one science fiction novel (*The Olympium of Bacchus 12*), two stand-alone action Suspense novels (*Shiko Unleashed* and *The Day of the Dead*), and two espionage/geo-political thrillers (*The Trinity Gambit* and *Codename: Mountbatten*). *Love's Second Chance, Stealing Love,* and *Love Lost, Love Found,* are William's first Adult Fiction/Contemporary Romance Novels.

William is a 5-time Royal Palm Literary Award winner: 2014 Second Place Unpublished Historical Fiction for *King's Ransom*, 2015 Second Place Unpublished Historical Fiction for *The Saga of Asbjorn Thorleikson*, 2017 Second Place Published Historical Fiction for *Arthur, King*, 2017 First Place Published Historical Fiction for *Nicaea – The Rise of the Imperial Church*, and 2017 First Place Published Science Fiction for *The Olympium of Bacchus 12*.

For more information about William Speir, please visit his website at WilliamSpeir.com.

Progressive Rising Phoenix Press is an independent publisher. We offer wholesale pricing and multiple binding options with no minimum purchases for schools, libraries, book clubs, and retail vendors. We offer substantial discounts on bulk orders and discounts on individual sales through our online store. Please visit our website at:
www.ProgressiveRisingPhoenix.com

If you enjoyed reading this book, please review it on Amazon, B & N, or Goodreads. Thank you in advance!

www.ingramcontent.com/pod-product-compliance
Lightning Source LLC
LaVergne TN
LVHW010258260326
834688LV00044B/1354